LIFEGUARD ON DUTY

U.S.S. SNOOK (SS-279)

Gerald R. Menefee

PublishAmerica
Baltimore

First printing

This is a work of fiction. Names, characters, places, and incidents either are the product of the author's imagination or are used fictitiously. Any resemblance to actual persons, living or dead, events, or locales is entirely coincidental.

PublishAmerica has allowed this work to remain exactly as the author intended, verbatim, without editorial input.

ISBN: 978-1-61582-786-2
PUBLISHED BY PUBLISHAMERICA, LLLP
www.publishamerica.com
Baltimore

Printed in the United States of America

Robert

Enjoy the read

[signature]

CHAPTER ONE

Lieutenant Jimmie Penn sat in the cockpit of his F4 Hellcat as the wings were being lowered into flight position. The winds gusted in his face and the flight deck before him pitched and yawed from the heavy seas this mighty aircraft carrier, U.S.S. Forrestal, had been experiencing for the past two days of near typhoon weather. And this was a better flight condition than anytime in the past four days. Penn pulled his leather helmet on and strapped it under his chin. He felt the stubble of a beard that had not been shaved for any of those four days when he and most of his pilot colleagues were too ill to want to bathe or shave. The Hellcat Squadron was born to fly and they were anxious to get airborne so they could do their thing.

They had spent the past forty-five minutes in the squadron ready room being briefed on the mission. They were carrying huge incendiary bombs strapped under the fuselages of their already bulky fighter aircraft. They were heading into Hachijo Jima, and atoll some 150 nautical miles south of Tokyo, where there was a known Japanese anti-aircraft emplacement. The Army Air Force brass were determined that by blowing up this military stronghold, a clear message would be sent to Tojo that the mainland of Japan was the next target and that he had better strongly consider the terms and conditions of surrender.

Part of the briefing had involved each pilot writing down the map coordinates to ditch points between the carrier and the atoll where the aircraft pilot could be assured of rescue if his aircraft was damaged too much to make it back to the carrier deck. Some of the coordinates were for surface ships that would be operating in the area that day. Other coordinates were for areas protected by submarines. The pilots often joked about whether the 'silent service' would in fact be where they said they would be. There was always a fear of what one could not see, and clearly the submarines seldom surfaced during the daytime. Given the choice, they had all agreed that they would head for a surface ship area.

The flight deck controllers were pointing their lighted sticks at Lt. Penn's plane now. He pulled back on the throttle to boost the fighter into motion and followed the deck crew's directions to place him on the port sided of the middle deck area. He locked his wheels and revved his engine. Then he released his wheel locks and felt the surge of power as the Hellcat leaped forward. The winds over the deck were so strong that he was off the deck long before he had passed the red warning stripe. He hit the control for raising the wheels into the fuselage and banked his plane slightly to the west.

As he gained altitude, he fell into formation with the other Hellcats and awaited the following planes that would make up the sixteen fighter-bombers that were in this mission. This was what he was born for. This is what he had trained for. He felt very much at home.

They flew in silence. They had been briefed that the enemy had become skilled at intercepting air communications and using the information to defend itself. There would be coded instructions from the group commander at the appropriate time, but each pilot knew his instructions and what was expected of him. It was a fifty-minute flight to their target area and it would be a quiet fifty minutes. Penn checked his instruments to assure himself that his plane was ready for the attack that was ahead of him. Everything checked out just fine.

The plans called for the group of sixteen to break into four units of four aircraft each when they neared the target area. They would attack from four different directions to confuse the gun emplacements. And their timing would be such that one plane from each direction would start the bombing run. As eight airplanes came in low to the ground, the other eight would make their bomb drops from high altitude. Likely the Japanese would wonder just what was hitting them, and believe that there were far more than sixteen planes involved. Mostly, the mission was intended to confuse the enemy so much that he would be ineffective in his defense.

Lt. Penn was assigned to one of the groups that would make a low level run at the targets. With approximately five minutes to go, and on the coded command of their flight leader, the eight planes broke formation and headed down to sea level. Then four planes broke off from the other four and headed off to starboard to make their run from the far side of the atoll. Penn and his three colleagues throttled back to give the second flight time to get around on the other side of the island before the designated strike time.

As the squadron leader gave the word, Penn reached over and pulled the lever that released the safety pins securing the large bomb in place. It was now held up to the fuselage only by two release pins that would blow away when the button was pushed on the top of the joystick that Penn used to navigate the Hellcat. He pushed the throttle into its stops giving the gutsy engine all the fuel it needed to maximize airspeed. A quick read of all the instruments told Penn that he was ready to engage the enemy.

The first planes into the foray were undetected. Their bombs made their targets and the planes were pulling up and away before the antiaircraft guns were able to load and fire. The second group of aircraft clearly had the enemy confused as the flack was spread all over the sky with no effectiveness. Penn was in the fourth and final group of planes to bomb the target. He watched ahead as the land gunfire came closer to the third set of Hellcats.

It was clear that they were doing their mission effectively. The bombs were causing great explosions and fires over the concentrated area of their targets. The smoke was billowing into the overcast sky and obliterating any chance that the gun emplacements could follow the planes in or out of their targets. Jimmie Penn felt his hand give a final push on the throttle just in case there was anything more there. He put his nose right on the point where he had seen the flash of gunpowder a moment ago. That was to be his target, and he was locked onto it. As he made his approach, he could see the opposite plane dropping his load and breaking off. Penn placed his right thumb over the button on the joystick and stared at his target. Nearing the landmass, he could now hear the boom of the flack and smell the acrid odor of the burning below.

Bomb away! He could feel his plane jerk as the heavy weight was dropped. He pushed the stick to the right and kept his low altitude. This was no time to go for the sky and lose airspeed. As his aircraft turned seaward he heard a slight staccato sound. He turned his head to see that a row of small caliber shells had tattooed his left wing. He did not feel any change in the aircraft controls and was still flying intact. He looked around to see the rest of the squadron running for the sea where they were to reform ten minutes away from the atoll target.

The mission appeared to be a success. The photographic reconnaissance planes would do a flyover later that morning and by late afternoon there would be pictures that the pilots could use in the debriefing of the carrier executives. For now, the paramount issue was the safe recovery of all sixteen planes back on the deck of the aircraft carrier.

As he gained altitude, Lt. Jimmie Penn realized that he had a problem. His first indication was visual. He could see some oil streaked where the bullets had penetrated his left wing. The controls to the aileron on that side were sluggish. He could guess that the hydraulic system that controlled that side of the plane had been damaged. He hoped that the damage was slight and he could make it back to the mother ship.

He called up the flight leader on his radio. "Flight leader, this is Red Four. I have some damage on my left wing. The hydraulics are going sluggish on me. So far it is only affecting the left side of the bird. Over."

"Red four, this is Flight Leader. I read you. Stay with us and keep me advised as to your status. We'll boost our speed to see if we can get you to Mother before things get worse. Flight Leader to all flight members. Let's go to 375 airspeed to see if we can get Red Four home quickly. My calcs tell me that we have enough fuel to make it. Out."

Penn could feel the lack of response in his controls as his airspeed rose. But he too knew that it was only a matter of minutes before he would lose enough hydraulic fluid so that none of the controls would operate. If he had to ditch, he would like to do so alongside the U.S.S. Forrestal.

As the minutes dragged by, Jimmie Penn became certain that he was not going to make it back to the Mother ship. The aileron controls were frozen and the electric pump was heating excessively. There would be a fire soon, and there was nothing he could do to disconnect the pump. "Flight Leader, this is Red Four. I am not going to make it back. I need to ditch. I have picked Sugar Bravo Three as my spot. Wish me luck. I'll see you guys soon."

The surface ship areas were too far to help Penn. He picked the map coordinates for one of the submarine areas directly in front of where he was headed and hoped that they would be sitting there awaiting him. He slowed his airspeed to make bailing out easier. Just as he was checking his parachute straps and feeling for the safety equipment that was clipped to his flight suit, a fire broke out in front of his right leg. This was it.

He pulled the canopy back to clear himself and shut the plane down as he made his jump. He cleared the tail nicely and pulled on the ripcord that released the parachute. Only then did he look downward at the sea below him. The hazy fog made the surface seem gray when it was usually an emerald green in this part of the world. There were small white caps in this area. He realized that he should be thankful that he wasn't in the storm area nearer the Forrestal.

Just before he hit the water, he slapped the quick release on his chute and dropped away from it. He remembered his flight instructor telling them about downed airmen drowning because they were caught up in their parachute shrouds in the sea. He bobbed back to the surface and looked around. Now where was that submarine?

Penn knew that, in addition to the standard area surveillance of the submarine, the carrier would contact Pearl Harbor and the submarine would receive a radio dispatch telling them of a downed aviator. He still would have preferred to see a ship on his way down to sea, but he clearly didn't have that choice. Another couple of minutes and he would have joined his aircraft that was at this time, heading for the bottom of the ocean out there in front of him somewhere. His 'Mae West' flotation collar was doing its job and the water wasn't cold. He guessed he could stay here until someone surfaced and found him. "Where the Hell are you?" he called out to the empty sea.

CHAPTER TWO

U p periscope," commanded Captain Emerson. "I want to search around to see what we have up there." The submarine and its crew had been submerged for ten hours, running at a depth of almost two hundred feet, evading the Japanese destroyers that were trying to locate them. Three different times during those ten hours, the depth charges were heard and felt as the surface hounds thought they smelled out their prey. Each time, however, the Snook had evaded the attack. Now it had been quiet for ninety minutes. Charles 'Skip' Emerson hoped that meant the destroyers had moved away from the area. He had brought his boat up to the 70-foot periscope depth.

The U.S.S. Snook had been at battle stations for the full ten hours. The officers and crew were weary to say the least. It was hot and humid aboard, the dank body odor of sweat permeating the ship. The cooks had not been able to prepare a meal during the long siege and the men were not in good humor as their stomachs reminded them of the hunger that joined their fear. The ship's batteries were being drained and were badly in need of recharging, but that would mean surfacing to run the engines and generators, a luxury that the Japanese had been denying.

As the periscope broke the surface of the sea, Skip Emerson was still in a squatting position as he rode the scope upward and twisted himself around the barrel 360 degrees to see if any of the enemy ships were anywhere near them. The sea surface was fairly calm, but it was still dark and the fog hampered any real view topside. "Everything looks clear topside, but let's wait a few minutes before we surface." To the Executive Officer Curt Thomas, Emerson said, "Take the scope XO, and keep a sharp eye for any movement out there."

"Aye, Captain," responded Thomas as he grabbed the horizontal control bars on the scope and swung it all round quickly to assure himself of no sightings.

"XO has the con," called the Skipper to the Control Room below. Then he reached over and took the microphone for the general announcing system in his hand. "Now hear this. Secure from General Quarters. Meal will be served in thirty minutes. The relieving detail is to eat first and take the place of those on watch while they eat. If everything stays quiet topside, we will be surfacing in one hour. Be prepared for manning the topside guns while we are charging our batteries. That is all, men." Skip turned to the XO and said, "Curt, I'm going below. Holler if you see anything and dive immediately. I'll be in the Wardroom."

As the Captain stepped down the ladder out of the Conning Tower into the Control Room, he reminded the Diving Officer and his Watch detail to stay alert in case an emergency dive was called for by the XO. Then he stepped through the hatchway leading forward into the Forward Battery compartment where, at this second level, the officers' staterooms and the Wardroom were situated. The waft of coffee greeted his nose and made his salivary glands become alert. He was reminded that he, too, had not eaten for twelve hours, although the excitement had kept his mind off food while he and his shipmates were evading the enemy lurking in the waters above.

The radio transmission from Pearl Harbor had been received almost fifteen hours prior, alerting the Snook that an airplane had been shot down in their area, and directing them to try to retrieve the aviator who was seen parachuting out of his plane before it crashed into the sea. Captain Emerson had immediately steamed to the coordinates that were received, vague as they were, and started a search pattern over the area. Starting with the map coordinates radioed to them, he and the XO set up a search process that expanded outward in grids of one-half mile. Almost five hours of searching the area, with no sight of the downed aviator, had gone by when they suddenly realized that their focus on the nearby surface had allowed three enemy destroyers to come over the horizon undetected. Both the Captain and Executive Officer were jarred awake by the explosion of a shell from the leading destroyer which landed not more than 100 yards off the port bow of the Snook.

"Clear the Bridge," screamed the Skipper. "Let's get out of here."

"Dive, dive. Now man your battle stations," he said over the announcing system. The klaxon immediately gave the warning throughout the boat with its "ooougha, ooougha" sound that alerted every crewmember to do exactly what they had each trained to do. In the Control Room the Chief of the Watch pulled the levers to open the flood valves, letting the air out of the ballast tanks that kept this huge vessel afloat. The bow and stern planes men were hydraulically lowering the planes that would control the angle and the level of the dive.

The Diving Officer called to the helmsman to ring up the order for 'All Ahead Full' to the Maneuvering Room where the electricians on watch were already shifting the propulsion from the generators attached to the engines for power on the surface, to the batteries that powered the motors connected to the screws while they were underwater.

"Answers 'All Ahead Full,'" called out the helmsman as soon as his enunciator registered the response.

The Diving Officer then informed the Captain who was in the Conning Tower, above, "We are at 200 feet per prior orders Skipper. Trim is proper and we are running at Ahead Full."

"Very well, Diving Officer," the Captain said as he came sliding down the ladder, placing his shoes on the outside of the hand rails to miss the steps of the ladder. "I have the dive," he ordered, thus relieving the Diving Officer who stepped back out of the way. "What are our conditions, Chief?" he asked the Watch Chief who had control of the hydraulic panels as ranking enlisted person on the dive.

"Green board, Skipper," called out Chief Engineman Sam Jones, "Everything is tight. We are rigged for dive in all compartments. Request you order depth charges condition, sir."

"Very well, Chief," responded the Captain as he pulled the hand-held microphone to his lips. "Rig for depth charges. Report your readiness to the Control Room." The quartermaster standing to the side of the

Captain wore a harness with a set of headphones to which a microphone was attached. The communications system was called 'sound powered' because it did not depend upon any outside electrical energy to make it work. The voice activated the carbon crystals in the microphone that transmitted the voice to others who were connected to the system's wiring in each compartment. The nature of the sound-powered communications system was such that no one heard anything without the earphones unlike the general announcing system that could be heard throughout the boat and was transmitted beyond its hull where others who were looking for them might also hear the sound. The quartermaster reported the responses from each compartment indicating that they had secured the valves and taken other actions to minimize damages caused by depth charges exploding near the boat. A direct hit would cause severe damage, but the crew hoped that they would not be found and that any depth charges to be dropped would be far enough away to only be heard and not felt.

"Quartermaster, announce 'Rig for Silent Running,'" said the Captain. As the message was passed over the phones, motors and pumps were secured that might also be heard by a sharp sonar operator on one of the enemy ships above. The most noticeable sound whirred to a stop as the air conditioning motors were turned off. The crew could immediately feel the humidity rise and the temperature start to climb. They hoped it would be a short attack.

CHAPTER THREE

Charles "Skip" Emerson, the Captain of the U.S.S. Snook, was a competent and wily leader. He was born in the small mid-western town of Fort Dodge, Iowa. His mother was a divorcee who moved Charles and his sister frequently as she feared that her ex husband's family would find the whereabouts of the children. With the matter of custody never brought to the courts, she lived in constant fear of losing her two babies. Charles, also known as "Skipper" and his sister, Jill, became close friends over the years of moving about. They would just meet new friends in their new neighborhood when they would be moved again. They soon realized that they were the only lasting friends they would have. With their mother working long hours as a hairdresser, they became dependent upon one another. Jill shortened her brother's nickname to "Skip" and he preferred it that way. He became known as "Skip" to school colleagues and others outside the family.

When the children were still pre-teenage, they were sent to live with their paternal aunt and grandmother. The aunt, a teacher who had never married, lived with the grandmother who had been widowed many years earlier. Charles and Jill were a godsend for these two ladies. And the stern, but loving, discipline of the two older ladies came at a time when it was sorely needed. Grandmother and aunt instilled values and purpose of life in the two siblings that would become their focus throughout their lives.

Skip Emerson thus grew up as a gregarious young man, anxious to meet people but unwilling to get too close to anyone. He excelled in sports, especially wrestling, where he contended in his weight class at the state level in high school and started at a small Iowa college on a partial scholarship he earned on the mats.

The Iowa Senator who was a friend of his aunt nominated Emerson to the U.S. Naval Academy. Skip was a mediocre student at Annapolis; more interested in sports that in academics. He learned about the seedy side of life through a few fellow students who took him along to the bars and introduced him to the ladies of the streets. He became legend among the midshipmen for his barroom brawls.

After graduation from the Academy, Ensign Skip Emerson was assigned aboard the battleship, U.S.S. Missouri. He hated the pomp and circumstance of life on a giant ship. He hated the formal atmosphere. He hated having to put on his dress uniform anytime he wanted to roam around the ship or go to the officers' mess for a meal. He heard about the elite corps of submariners and applied for Submarine School at New London, Connecticut.

Shortly before he gained his full stripe as Lieutenant Junior Grade he received his orders to Submarine School. He was elated as he packed his belongings and bid goodbye to his buddies on the Mighty Mo. As he walked down the gangplank, he vowed he would never again do duty on a big surface ship.

Submarine School was full of surprises. There was so much to learn that it was like going back to the university for postgraduate work. The faculty had high expectations for each student. Failure to make the grade would mean being assigned back to a surface ship or shore station at the discretion of the senior faculty members. Skip Emerson had nightmares about being sent back to the U.S.S. Missouri. He drove himself out of this fear. Besides, Groton, Connecticut and its neighbor, New London, were isolated from any large city so it was not easy to find an anonymous bar or place to pick up on of the ladies of the streets. Those escapades were saved for the few available weekends when Skip and his buds would catch a bus to New York City, some two hours away.

The war was heating up in the Pacific. The Washington brass was building the submarine forces that were to be used to repel the Japanese off the major islands in which they were gaining a foothold. Upon graduation, LTJG Charles Emerson was assigned to a transit crew that was taking a brand new submarine through the Panama Canal to Hawaii. He thought his wildest dreams were being answered. He called his family in Iowa to tell them the news.

"Hey, Sis," he said as Jill answered the telephone, "Guess what? I get to go to the land of hula skirts where I will be stationed on one of the submarines at Pearl Harbor. Isn't that exciting? We are leaving next week on a new boat that will take us along the Atlantic seaboard, through the Gulf of Mexico, across the Panama Canal, and into the Pacific Ocean where we will steam on to Hawaii. I think I've died and gone to heaven."

The only noteworthy event in the transit was Panama, where Skip and two buddies were ashore in Colon, on the Caribbean side of the canal, while their ship awaited its turn to enter the canal. A gang of locals, bent upon relieving these naval officers of their money, surrounded the three on a side street and made their demands for wallets and watches. In spite of the machete knives being brandished by these fierce looking hoods, Skip threw the first blow knocking one of the robbers to the ground. What followed that act has never been described in detail, but two of the naval officers, including Skip Emerson, got slashed by the knives pretty severely before the gang took off to find another, less combative, target. It took thirty stitches at the local Army Hospital to sew Skip's shoulder and neck back together. And it ended their shore leave. No sooner had they reported back to their submarine but they were underway to enter the Canal.

Thus started a career and personality for Charles "Skip" Emerson. His dedication to his profession at sea was unquestioned. He was a quick study, and always alert to new strategies. His shipmates trusted him. They knew that he would be bold in the defense of his country. They came to know that he cared about each of them. He was also followed by the stories of his capers on shore. He continued to be a brawler when he drank too much. And he continued to be a carouser ashore, looking for the seamy ladies that frequented the downtown bars in Honolulu just as he had sought them in Baltimore.

Emerson quickly rose in rank through service as an Engineering

Officer on two war patrols and Executive Officer status shortly after receiving his promotion to full Lieutenant. As the flood of new boats arrived at Pearl Harbor for deployment there and in Australia, there were many new commands awarded to those who showed their strengths in boldness of leadership. Charles Emerson headed that class.

Skip Emerson had met Curt Thomas when they crewed together on the U.S.S. Argonaut the prior year. Curt, who graduated from the Academy the year after Skip, was Engineering Officer while Skip was the XO. They had developed a friendship that went beyond the submarine and the Navy they served. Both men lived in Bachelor Officers' Quarters on the base at Pearl Harbor. When out of uniform, Curt was as straight laced as Skip was wild. His tempering personality was something that Skip needed and Curt could talk to Skip bout his antics. Skip was sure that Curt would have his own submarine soon, and tried to give him every opportunity to show his mettle on the Snook.

CHAPTER FOUR

Sixty minutes after the Captain had left the Con to his XO the telephone in the Wardroom buzzed. The Captain, alone with his third cup of coffee, picked up the handset.

"Captain, this is XO. We remain clear topside. I'd like your permission to surface, call the gun crew topside, and start the battery charge. We are down to about 20 minutes of battery power left."

"O.K. Curt, but have the gun crews help with the watch. We don't want anymore of those surprises like the last one. And resume the search pattern for the downed aviator, even though I think we would have found him earlier if the data we received were any good." With that the Captain put the headset back and resumed his cogitation. He had written some notes to himself that he wanted to polish and present to the Commander, Submarine Forces Pacific (ComSubPac) when they returned to Pearl. The Snook needed one of the new radar units that were being installed for surface detection of ships. If he had one, he would not have been caught off guard by the three escorts that had almost been his undoing and that caused him to interrupt the aviator search for almost twelve critical hours. Beyond that, he pondered how to get a better and quicker fix on exactly where the pilots were crashing into the sea. Even though the water was warm, these seas were full of enemy ships and sharks, and the skies often were filled with fog that made visual searching impractical. If an aviator could not be found within a few hours of his crash, he was probably not going to be found alive.

Drained emotionally and physically from the past dozen hours, Skip Emerson decided that he would catch some sleep. After letting the XO know that he would be in his cabin, he hung up his shirt and took off his shoes. He loosened his trousers but was unwilling to undress further in case he was needed immediately. His sleep could be interrupted at any moment while they were on the surface. The only time he got any sustained sleep was while they were submerged. That meant many of the days of operation when the daylight forced them to stay submerged and running submerged meant they would only move at slow speeds. They made their fast surface transits during the cover of night.

Emerson jerked awake thinking he heard a voice. He waited momentarily and assured himself that it was all in his head. He looked at his watch. He had been asleep for three hours as though in a drug induced trance. He stretched his six foot two inch body out of the berth he called his home away from home, and stood up. He pulled down his compartment sink and splashed some water on his face. He felt surprisingly good.

He called the steward to bring two cups of coffee to the bridge for Mr. Thomas and himself, and headed aft to the Control Room where he greeted the Watch Chief on his way up the ladder through the Conning Tower and on to the bridge. "Captain to the Bridge," he called out as he stuck his head up onto the wooden deck plating that formed the bridge area at the front of the sail.

"Good evening, Captain," greeted the XO. "Everything has been quiet up here. Did you get that rest you needed?"

"You bet I did. I expected to nap, but my body and mind decided differently. How is the battery charge coming along? Did you sight any indication of the aviator?"

"The battery charge was just completed. We are fully charged and ready for propulsion on engines or batteries. No signs of any kind to indicate there ever was anyone in the sea around here. No floating debris from the airplane. And certainly no sign of human life. The fog has closed in twice since we surfaced and has hampered any kind of serious search at distance. We closed in our search pattern during the fog, though, so we wouldn't depend on distance sightings. I'm afraid we have struck out on the search."

"God, Curt. There has to be a better way, don't you think? We get radio messages from Pearl that are often several hours late and then the map coordinates get scrambled through the multiple handling of data. It reminds me of that game of 'telephone' we used to play as kids where you would say something to the person to your left and the message would be repeated around a circle until it got back to you. Then the person to your right would say what you said to start the game. Any similarities were purely coincidental and the more people in the chain of communications, the worse the message got scrambled."

"I agree Skip, there must be a better way. Why couldn't we get a radio like the airplanes have and connect it to one of our antennas? If we disconnect the transmitter, we can't be expected to respond, but we could hear directly from the aircraft carrier or the pilot who was bailing out. We could have the exact map coordinates, immediate notification, and without the communication tree that causes some errors."

"My God, Curt. I think you have the solution. Why hasn't someone thought of that before? What a great idea. I think we should code your thoughts and transmit them to SubPac at our next radio traffic time this evening. If we can get hold of one of those radios and get a surface radar installed while we are at Pearl, we can try to become real lifeguards on our next patrol."

"Lifeguards, that's rich!" exclaimed Thomas. "I've never heard that expression before, but it really is what they want us to be, isn't it? Why don't we package our proposal as 'Operation Lifeguard? Will you buy co-ownership with me, Skip?"

"It would be my pleasure, but be assured that I will give you the credit you deserve if SubPac will buy into the radio receiver idea. In fact, I'd like to relieve you to go below and start coding the transmission so we can send it when we are expected to contact the sub headquarters in about two and a half hours."

"I'm going to secure from the search effort, too," added the CO, "If we haven't found any trace of the pilot by now, we won't in another few hours. It is important that we be on station tomorrow. Hopefully, to observe ship movements that we can intercept."

CHAPTER FIVE

Yeoman Smith, ask Commander Walker to bring the file on Lieutenant Commander Charles Emerson to my office for a discussion at 1045 hours, please," said Captain Phillip Brannigan into his intercom.

"Will do, Captain." Chief Smith called the Public Information Office and left a message with the secretary that Commander Walker and the file were needed.

Phil Brannigan had been reading the decoded message from the U.S.S. Snook. The proposal for 'Operation Lifeguard' was a fantastic idea, and a practical one at that. He wanted to know what kind of guy this Emerson was before he went to Admiral Pennington for permission to move ahead on its implementation. Captain Brannigan knew that Jim Walker had information on all the submarine commanders in his files.

Commander James Walker had made his professional career in data and information. Beyond the printed information, Jim Walker was a treasure chest of informal info about people and places. He used that information carefully and judiciously whether he was dealing with local and national press services, or with a Naval colleague. Of course, Captain Brannigan was his superior officer at SubPac headquarters, but more than that, Phil Brannigan had earned Walker's trust through their having worked together ever since the start of the war. They had both been pre-war submarine skippers and knew the skills and qualifications necessary. The were masters at perpetuating the "Silent Service" approach to their branch of the United States Navy, while giving the appearance of wanting to work openly with the media.

Jim Walker had admired Phil Brannigan's handling of difficult matters, recalling to himself how Brannigan had worked with the Senior Editor, now Editor In Chief, of the Honolulu Breeze. The case had involved the U.S.S. Trout that had managed the removal of the national treasury from the Philippines just after the start of World War II, when it was becoming apparent that the Japanese were planning a massive assault on the Philippines Islands. The reporter, a guy named J. Denton Edwards, had refused to stop snooping around and was fabricating a story that could have brought serious political and military consequences. Captain Brannigan had met with the Honolulu Breeze and threatened to involve the White House. The reporter was fired and had not been heard from since.

Jim Walker chuckled to himself as he reviewed the file on LCDR Charles Emerson, captain of the U.S.S. Snook. This man had an impeccable record while on duty and at sea, but had become almost legend for his antics while ashore. He glanced at his watch and realized that he had better get moving if he wanted to resume his exercise fitness program by taking the stairs up to Captain Brannigan's office and avoid the jingle of the elevator bells calling to him.

"Come on in, Jim," Brannigan called to him as he saw Walker approaching his open door. "Close the door, please. We have some serious business before us. Read this."

He handed the decoded message to Walker and watched his expressions as he read it. These two men had worked together for three years now, and had come to read each others expressions. Of course, when they were out on official business, each had learned to mask those expressions, but in the sanctity of the headquarters building, their real feeling were seldom masked. Brannigan like what he saw on Walker's face.

"What an incredible idea. It is so practical that I am only amazed that we, or someone else, have not thought of this before. It removes the problem of second- or third-hand information, and makes the data immediately available to the subs on station in the area where the emergency is taking place. If the submarine is on the surface, or close enough to let their radio whip antenna touch the surface, they will receive the communications directly from the airplane or the controller on the aircraft carrier."

"Exactly right, Jim. Now, before I brief Admiral Pennington and seek his go-ahead on this 'Operation Lifeguard' I want to know what kind of guy LCDR Emerson is. Is he credible? Should we be concerned that he can't bring this idea off after we get permission?"

"Funny you should ask, Phil. Skip Emerson has an outstanding record as a submarine commander. He has sunk more than his share of tonnage, and has completed four war patrols. But his history ashore is badly blemished. In fact, he is probably the most talked about skipper in the bars and the O Club. He has never seemed to get over his record as a college wrestler and has a short fuse after he has had a few drinks. He was involved in a fracas in Panama just out of Sub School while transiting a boat here, in which he got his throat cut. The Naval contingent in Panama hopes he never comes back there. It took them several months to get the locals quieted down after that mishap. We have had to intervene on three occasions here in Hawaii or he would have ended up in the local jail. And he likes women, lots of women. But he is a dedicated leader when he is 'on task.'"

"I'd like to have him work with us and the brass over at Hickam Army Air Force Base on the implementation of his proposal. Do you think we can keep him on the straight and narrow?"

"We can sure try, Phil. I'm willing to work with him if you are. Maybe one of your 'sonny boy' speeches would be appropriate if we bring him into this. I also understand that his XO is a crackerjack engineer with an electronics background. Perhaps he is the one to involve. Or we could use both and have this Lieutenant Thomas keep a rein on Emerson."

"I like that idea best, Jim. If the Admiral agrees, we will recall the Snook and put both the Co and XO to work in outfitting the Snook for a trial run on 'Operation Lifeguard.'"

CHAPTER SIX

As the U.S.S. Snook was being secured to Finger Pier 3 at Pearl Harbor, a messenger stepped across the gangplank. Saluting the flag, he turned to the Officer of the Deck, "Sir, I have a message for Captain Emerson. May I leave it with you?"

The OOD signed for the message and told the messenger he could leave. Then the OOD turned to the Duty Petty Officer who accompanied him on deck. "Gunner," he said, "Take this below to the Skipper."

"Aye, Aye, Sir. Can I bring you a cup of java when I come back up?"

"That would be appreciated, Gunner. A little cream and no sugar, if you will."

Knocking on the wall at the entrance to the Wardroom, the Petty Officer handed the message to the Captain. "This was just delivered topside as the lines were being doubled and secured to the pier. The OOD had me bring it right down to you, Sir."

"Thanks for doing that." Skip Emerson quickly read the message to see if there was any reply required. "That will be all, Gunner. There is no response needed."

Gunner left the doorway and stuck his head into the Officers' Pantry. "Hey, Stew. Can I get two cups of that great coffee of yours?" Gunner knew that the only way he could get a cup of good coffee was to bring one to the OOD. Enlisted men were required to get their coffee in the mess hall. That coffee was O.K. but there was always something special about the coffee the officers had. He was sure he would enjoy this cup. He went into the Forward Torpedo Room and climbed up through the Escape Chamber onto the forward deck of the boat. From there, it was only a few feet to the place where the brow gangplank had been placed.

Gunner wondered to himself, as he handed one of the cups to the OOD, about the name 'gangplank.' He could envision planks thrown across from a dock to a ship to let people carry things across. But this 'gangplank' was made of aluminum, strong and still lightweight. One sturdy person could swing it about on the deck or pier. It had a set of large wheels mounted on the dockside and vertical stanchions on one side with covered light chains running horizontal to the deck to allow anyone to steady themselves while crossing. Gunner had watched many civilian visitors over the months hold on to these as they might grip a banister on their home stairway as they made the transition from the steadiness of the dock to the rolling movement as a ship stirred the water in the channel.

As the XO stuck his head into the Wardroom to assure the Skipper that everything was secured, he was asked to grab a cup of coffee and join the Captain. "It seems that SubPac thinks your idea for a radio transmitter has merit. The Chief of Staff, Captain Brannigan, wants us to come up the hill tomorrow morning at 0900 to meet with him and a few of his colleagues on the Admiral's staff. I'm impressed with their quick reaction. I've heard from others that ideas sent to the brass just die there."

"Hey, I'm looking forward to that meeting. I've never been to ComSubPac headquarters. That alone ought to be worth the trip. Why don't we plan to meet this evening to discuss the plan so that I don't step on any toes tomorrow?" Thomas was really thinking that an evening might keep Emerson on base so he didn't spend the entire night carousing.

"What? Our first night back in port and you want to spend it thinking about business? Come on, Thomas, what's with you? Oh! I get it. You are trying to ground me so I will be fit for the meeting aren't you?"

"I've got to admit, Skip. I'd like to have my first meeting with SubPac folks get off to a positive start. Besides, we have all the reports from the other officers that we need to wrap together for the patrol, while it is fresh in our minds, don't we? And won't it be more fun to celebrate tomorrow night when we can include our victory with SubPac on top of the successful patrol?"

"Yeh, I guess you are right. All right, let's plan to meet at the BOQ at 1930 hours." With that, Skip Emerson arose and headed out of the Wardroom aft to take a look at things to make sure for himself, before going ashore, that everything was in order.

Curt Thomas sat in the Wardroom wondering if he had been too direct with Skip. He did not want to alienate his boss, but he was sure that everyone afloat, and probably SubPac too, knew about the skirmishes that Skip Emerson was infamous for. He really did want to set a positive image for himself, if not Emerson. After all, he wanted to have his own command of a submarine one of these days.

The next morning, Lieutenant Thomas and Lieutenant Commander Emerson, dressed in their 'undress whites' headed for their meeting with the staff at ComSubPac. They used the jeep that was assigned to each boat while it was in port. They had put the windshield down against the flat hood of the jeep to enjoy the sweetness of fresh air on the drive. The roadway up to the headquarters building was narrow, not made for much traffic. The Hibiscus banked on each side were stunning in their bright red petals and long yellow stamen against the lush dark green foliage that formed their beds. The sweet smell made Skip reminisce about the last time he held one of the local beauties in his arms.

They were logged in at the front desk and introduced to Chief Smith, the enlisted aide to Captain Brannigan, who led them up the stairway to the third floor office of the Chief of Staff. They could see the mahogany paneled entrance to Admiral Pennington's suite just down the hallway as they turned into Captain Brannigan's waiting area. This office was not quite as sumptuous as the Commander in Chief's but it was a whole lot nicer than anything either of these submarine officers had seen recently. Brannigan greeted them at his office door. "We will be meeting down the hall in the Admiral's Conference Room, gentlemen. Please tell the Chief how you like your coffee. We have a special brew that I think you will enjoy. I remember how I used to yearn for a good cup of coffee on those long patrols we made back in the S Boats that I knew so well. Of course, you have a lot of creature comforts on your fleet boats that we never had, but I know that things are cramped for you. And every time we come up with some new electronics device, I keep asking our engineering staff where we are going to put it."

Skip Emerson noted the craggy, while still handsome, features of the smiling face that spoke to him. He would be willing to bet that Phillip Brannigan had been something of a ladies' man in his hay day, too. "Thank you for inviting us, Captain. I hope that you have had a chance to consider our proposal. Really, I want to give full credit to Mr. Thomas here. Curt and I were lamenting the inability to find a downed airman on this last patrol when he came up with the idea that we forwarded to you."

"Yes, I have, Commander. But first, let's get seated and I'll introduce the staff that been analyzing your proposal and others relating to this problem of ours." Captain Brannigan then introduced each staff member around the table as the stewards served coffee to all in attendance and placed several silver platters with sweet rolls on the table. "Gentlemen, I want to make the most of this opportunity. As our allied forces get closer and closer to the mainland of Japan, there is more and more resistance to the air attacks, and there are just more aircraft coming along. We are diverting forces from the European theatre to the Pacific. So we have more aircraft in the air, both from land bases and carriers, and the Japanese are concentrating their aircraft back at the homeland.

"We have all been frustrated with the prior arrangements wherein submarine commanders were assigned a patrol area and asked to be on the lookout for downed aircraft. The aircraft squadrons have been told of the assigned patrol areas, but the arrangement has not worked. The pilots fear ditching their aircraft in the designated areas because they can't see our submarines and are concerned that we might have left. Indeed, in many instances, enemy surface craft have caused our subs to have to move away. The wing commanders are as concerned as we are about the amount of time their pilots and other crewmembers are in the sea. They might be sighted by enemy men-of-war or worse yet, by the nemeses of the sea—the sharks. As a result, the pilots try to ditch near a surface ship where they have a better chance. We know that they often do not make it to a suitable point and are lost at sea.

"I have invited Lieutenant Commander Emerson, the Captain of the U.S.S. Snook, and his Executive Officer, Lieutenant Curt Thomas, to join us this morning. These two warriors have submitted a proposal that is of great interest for it may provide a solution to the problem I have just outlined. Commander, my engineering staff has read your proposal, but I would like for you to start off by reviewing it with us. Then we will get into some discussions."

"Thank you, Captain Brannigan. It is a pleasure to meet with you all this morning. Even though I might rather be lying on Waikiki Beach soaking up some of the sun that we miss at sea, my Executive Officer and I are pleased to have this opportunity. And might I add that we are impressed that you have taken the time to study our proposal and respond so quickly. I would like to set the stage for those of you who have not had the opportunity to play 'lifeguard' before, and then I am going to ask Lieutenant Curt Thomas to brief you on what was really his idea.

"The current modus calls for us to take a general position, usually as a cluster of submarines, and those positions are given to the Army Air Corps. There are many things that you will all remember can cause a sub to not be on station at a given time. Most often, we are driven away by enemy men-of-war or wander out of the area pursuing enemy shipping in hope that we can sink one of the enemy ships. Even when we are on station, weather conditions get worse as we get closer to the land masses from Hokkaido Island in the north to Kyushu Island in the south. And there are other times when we cannot run on the surface and may miss the ditching of the aircraft altogether. With that reminder, let me now turn this presentation over to Curt Thomas, who has shown his knowledge of engineering in the past and will be one of the premier submarine commanders in the future."

"Thanks, Skipper. I just want to say, without sounding trite about it, that serving with submarine commanders like Skip Emerson, is what stimulates a crew to do its very best. When I first went to Skip with this idea, it was pretty rough. But he encouraged me to work out the proposal you have seen and to critically think about all the ramifications of what we are trying to accomplish out there." Curt Thomas went on explaining the proposal merits and many of the questions that remained unanswered.

Commander Fleming, the Engineering Staff Executive interjected, "Excuse me, gentlemen, but have you thought about how you are going to receive any radio communications when you are under water? It is one thing if you can hang 60 feet and extend the radio whip antenna, but that is rather impractical."

"We are not sure about this," responded Lt. Thomas, "but our Chief Radioman thinks that a flexible ribbon like antenna could be played out so that it floated on the surface. Such an antenna could stay on the surface even if we were down at 100 feet and would be small enough that it would practically be invisible from the surface. That is what could make this whole proposal work, if such a thing could be made to work. It would have to be expendable because we might need to cut it loose if we were evading surface contacts or if it got wrapped around something on or near the surface."

Commander Fleming turned to his staff, "What do you think? Could such an antenna be made to work?"

Lieutenant James Gault turned to his superior officer. "I think that is an incredible idea. I have seen some mention in literature of a floating antenna, but never thought about it as an application to this problem. Yes, I think something could be devised and I would like to work with these submarine officers and their radioman chief on the idea."

Captain Brannigan broke into the conversation, having been quiet for the 90 minutes during which all these discussions were taking place. "Gentlemen, I think that we have something. I want to form a task force, including all of us here, to work through this idea. I'd like Commander Fleming to be the project officer from my office, and I would hope that our two Snook officers will be a vital part of the team. Let's plan to meet one week from today with answers to as many questions as we can devise. I also want to start conversations with the Army Air Corps on this matter. I would like for Fred Fleming and Skip Emerson to meet with me right after this meeting so we can set up an appointment with some people at Hickam AFB. We are adjourned with my greatest thanks to all of you, and my wishes for our success. Remember that you are carrying the authority of Admiral Pennington. Invoke that authority any time you need to if a shop or shipyard person balks at giving you top priority. That is all, gentlemen."

With that, the meeting was adjourned. Curt Thomas and Jim Gault were immediately gathered in a corner talking about the concept of a floating antenna. Commander Fleming and Skip Emerson followed Captain Brannigan down the hall to his office. When they got there, Fleming asked if he could be excused for a couple of minutes to make an urgent call, after which he would meet Brannigan and Emerson in the Chief of Staff's office.

"Come on up, Skip," said Brannigan. "We need to talk about something first, anyway. We'll see you, Fred, in ten minutes.

"Well, Skip, it appears that you and young Curt Thomas have come up with what may be the real answer to this damning dilemma that we have been confronting for so long. I liked the openness of Thomas and Gault on the matter of the floating antenna. I hope you guys can provide the field orientation that this project needs. Frankly, some of us, including Fred Fleming, have been on the shore so long that we may have lost touch with what you really need out there at sea and at war. But I am sure we can work that out.

"What I want to talk about, first, is you on-shore relationships, Skip. We cannot afford to get this major project underway only to find that you are too tied up with some skirts or too bruised up to participate. I know something of your past history on the beach. We have all been ignoring your escapades because you are one damn fine submarine skipper. But this project is based on land and a portion of the effort is away from the sub. What I want to know, right now, is can you stay with us on this?"

"Well, I will give you credit for not mincing words, Captain. I know that I suffer from the urges of all single men and that I have allowed my temper to get out of control while I am not on duty. I think that I can consider this project as 'on duty' time and that will keep my nose clean. I appreciate your clearing the air for us on this matter."

"O.K. then we will not speak of this again. Let me know if you need some reinforcement of this topic, Skip. I will not initiate any further discussion until or unless I hear from you."

Captain Brannigan was making a call to the Commander, Hickam Army Air Force Base when Fred Fleming returned to the office. When Brannigan hung up, he announced that the three of them and Emerson's XO would meet tomorrow at 1030 hours at the Hickam AFB executive offices. Brannigan would alert the commanders of the carrier air group and his counterpart at the Commander In Chief, Pacific Fleet, for their representation. The problems for Naval Air would be similar to those for the bombers of the Army Air Force, but Brannigan realized that the radio equipment would be easier to requisition for the Naval air units than for the Army air units. He wanted to make sure that any serious planning exposed the most extensive problems first.

He was reasonably sure that he could predict the positive response from the Naval air and carrier groups; he was less sure about the cooperation of the Army, where the old brass had witnessed a major organizational rift when the Army Air Corps became the Army Air Force. What had been decentralized air support to ground forces had become a centralized air force from the ground troops.

"In the meantime," Brannigan said, addressing Emerson and Fleming, "I'd like for you two guys to try to start some discussions with the Radio Shop over at the Sub Base to see what it will take to get a model of a floating whip antenna."

"Captain Brannigan, I'd like to assign my XO and Chief Radioman to that task, sir. They have already had some informal communications with the base and will facilitate it faster if we don't stick our noses in. The Sub Base shops have a habit of becoming very cautious and structured when SubPac is involved. Otherwise, we work very quickly and easily on less documentation when its just them and us."

"Yeh, you're right, Skip. I'll expect you to keep a close eye on things and we four will have a discussion tomorrow after the big meeting at Hickam, about directions. I'll see you both tomorrow morning then." With that, Brannigan walked to the door of his office and bid goodbye to his guests.

After talking about what they expected to happen the next morning, Skip Emerson said goodbye to Fleming and strolled out the headquarters front entrance while Fleming headed up the stairway toward his office.

Finally, Skip felt that he had secured some free time for himself. He really did feel that Brannigan, Fleming, and he should stay out of the way of Thomas and his crew, but he also was anxious to cut a little room for himself. He hadn't had a relaxing evening since they went to sea five weeks before. He was overdue for a little "R&R" which he considered "rum and rubdown" instead of the norm, and he knew just where to fulfill his needs.

CHAPTER SEVEN

He stopped by the Batchelor Officers' Quarters (BOQ) just long enough to grab a couple of shirts and slacks. Then he headed his jeep toward Honolulu and Waikiki Beach where he would sign into a room at the Royal Hawaiian Hotel. All the submariners were given free board and room at this magnificent hotel on the beach, while they were in port.

Skip checked in and dropped his gear in the room. He changed into a swimsuit and, grabbing a towel from the bathroom, headed out the side door and walked around the building to the beachfront. Finding an open spot, he spread out his towel and left his sunglasses atop it while he raced for the surf. The warm water was a cool relief from the sand that was trying to blister his feet. He was set to dive into the next breaker when one knocked him head over heels backward. It had been too long since he had tried that little maneuver, and he had forgotten to angle his dive. The force of the breaker proved to be stronger coming onto the shore than the direct force of his dive forward.

As he lay there trying to decide whether to laugh or cry, Skip became aware of a soft melodious voice to his left. "Are you all right? Do you need some assistance?" The voice was so soft he thought he was imagining it. He turned his head to the left and saw a bronze vision about ten feet behind him on the dry sand. She was a gorgeous dark skinned goddess. He decided to play out this fantasy, if that is what it was.

"I think I'm O.K., but I'm going to reserve judgment for a couple of minutes. Right now I feel like a damn fool tourist who has been given my comeuppance by the very ocean that earns me my living. In the meantime, would you care to soothe my brow? I don't suppose that you are also a nurse, are you?" Skip waited to see if there would be a response or whether he was just dreaming this whole thing.

"As a matter of fact, I am. Lieutenant Junior Grade Nancy Jones at your service. Called Nurse Nancy by many, I prefer 'Nance' among my friends. And who but a friend would do such a stupid thing as you just did?" She smiled and got up to walk toward where Skip was still lying. He thought he would never get over that face, but the minute she started toward him, Skip focused on the swaying hips and saunter that was all her own. He pinched his leg hard, hoping that it would not cause him simply to wake up to nothing. But she was real and she was there, kneeling beside him now.

"I think that, other than some minor abrasions, you will be stiff for a couple of days and no worse off for you adventure. Would you care to come up on the sand and join me? What do I call you?"

"Skip Emerson—just call me Skip. And I'd love to join you just as soon as I wash some of this sand off me." Skip got' up and walked into the surf, joined by Nance, where they dipped into warm water. "I've got to tell you that I have never done that trick before. I have been away for so long that I have forgotten how to slant dive into the surf. The locals make it look so easy, and I showed the world how the tourists do it. Okay, I'm ready to join you now. Let me just get my towel and meet you at yours."

Skip started toward his towel but he couldn't take his eyes off Nance. Wow! Am I lucky or what? Who is this nymph? He decided to play it cool as long as he could. Tripping over a piece of coral mostly buried in the sand, he was jarred back into the present. He walked over and picked up his towel and glasses. He suddenly remembered how hot the sand was under foot. He raced over and spread his towel and flopped down on its insulating feel.

"So, Nurse Nancy, what do you do when not attending to fools on the beach?"

"Well, I am attached to Tripler Army Hospital right now. I've only been here in Hawaii for three weeks and will try to get transferred to the base dispensary at Pearl Harbor as soon as I can. Tripler is so big and impersonal that I'm uncomfortable with it. I was born and raised on Guam and trained to be a nurse there. When the war broke out, I signed up presuming that I would stay on Guam. My specialty is radiation treatment so when I was told that there was a critical need here, I jumped at the opportunity to live in Hawaii for a few years. And I love it. The people are friendly and being in the Navy has its benefits. The locals are very appreciative that we are protecting them from further attacks or invasion. They know that the United States would never let that happen. The way that the forces were mobilized after the attack on Pearl Harbor proved to everyone in Hawaii that the mainlanders really do care. How about you, Skip? What are you doing here?"

"I'm captain of a submarine based at Pearl. I graduated from the Academy four years ago and went through Submarine School as soon as I could. I have been at the right place at the right time and gotten all the military breaks I could expect. I was in the first group of my class to make Lieutenant Commander and was the second in my class to get command of a submarine. I love what I am doing, and am convinced that submarines will be the undoing of the Japanese forces. We are effectively cutting off the troop movements and materials that must be imported to Japan to keep its war efforts going on. I live in the BOQ at Pearl Harbor, but we are given rooms here at the Royal Hawaiian when we are in port. This is the first chance I've had, since we came back into port yesterday, to get a little time to myself. And I feel very fortunate to have met such a lovely lady so early in the day."

"Well the feeling in mutual, Skip," Nance said. "You can't imagine how fresh it feels to make an approach myself. I can't go anywhere on this beach without the catcalls. But that all stops when I have a companion. Then the gentlemen behave like gentlemen. So I have learned to pick out someone I would like to talk to and quickly make contact. When you came running down toward the water, I said to myself that I would like to visit with you. You have that freshness, too. You weren't ogling the girls first. You were intent on enjoying the water and soaking up some sun. Speaking of which, you should have some oil on to protect your skin.

You know, the sun emits radiation not unlike that which I deal with every day in the hospital. Some of the ultra violet rays can be harmful. I have some oil here that you should apply to keep you skin protected from burn, and from drying too."

"Okay, Nance. Can I ask you to do my back? I can never get it spread evenly. I'll do yours in return."

"I'm fine for now, thanks. I'll be glad to rub some oil on you back. I'll try to be careful around those abrasions on your right shoulder. Boy you are a mess of scratches aren't you?" Nance proceeded to spread oil on Skip's back and rub it around to cover all the skin that wasn't too badly scratched up.

Skip tried not to show his excitement at her touch. He sat before her, cross-legged. He knew that he couldn't lie down right now or the erection he was having would surely give him away and might turn her off. Things were going well and Skip had resolved not to push too quickly. As she rubbed the oil around, Skip felt the muscles start to relax. This was heaven on Earth. When she had finished, he said, "Thanks, Nance. You cannot imagine how soothing that felt. More than the oil on my back, your hands on my back made me realize how tense I have been since we returned from this past war patrol. I cannot allow myself to show any of the tensions while we are underway, so it always shows up afterward. It is my body's way of reacting to the war and my command."

"Why don't you just lie down on your towel and let me give you a quick rub down? I do this for a living, you know. I've done so many for patients that I should be getting pretty good by now."

Skip could feel the five weeks of tension flowing out of his body as Nance's trained hands did their magic. How could he be so lucky as to find this beauty in his first two minutes on the beach? Where was this meeting destined to go? "You know," he said turning his head toward her, "I cannot remember when I've felt better. I'd like to buy us a drink. Are you ready to go up to the bar? Or would you prefer that I go get us something?"

"Let's walk up to the bar. I think I've had enough for the day. I have to watch out that I don't get too much sun or I really get dark skin. And you probably had better get out before you get burned to a crisp."

They picked up their belongings and headed up across the sand and on to the walkway that runs the length of Waikiki Beach from the park and zoo where the coastline turns south toward Diamond Head, to the west extreme where the beach ends with a sharp turn toward the Alawaie Canal.

The bar in the Royal Hawaiian was quiet this early afternoon. They found a table for two near an open window overlooking the beach. It was a setting fit for the paradise of lovers. The cooling trade winds blew through the open window and made the palm trees sing their whispered song. The plumerias and orchids filled the air with their sweet scent. The couple sat silently sipping their rum coladas, each gazing into the eyes of the other.

"This is what I dreamed about on those hot sweaty nights of my youth," started Nance. "When we kids would gather for the evening, after our household chores were done, each neighborhood had its place where we knew the others would come. And we would while away the hours dreaming out loud, vocalizing what we hoped the future would be for us. We had very little awareness of what the rest of the World was like, but we had our vision of what we hoped was out there. I had this recurring dream about being a nurse on a far-away island where I would meet this tall, handsome man who would sweep me off my feet. And we would live happily ever after. Did you ever have dreams like that, Skip?"

"When I was growing up in that little town in Iowa, being raised by an aunt and grandmother, my sister and I would talk about the future when we would each have our own family and would never leave our children. I can't remember that it mattered much where we were, but we missed having real parents so much that we focused mostly on that part of what we wanted to have and to be."

"My parents are good people. You would like them. Daddy is a fisherman as are most of the islanders. Mommy works hard at providing a good home for her husband and her family. Things are not easy on a small island. There are none of the luxuries that I have seen here. There are no refrigerators and no ice. There are no electric washing machines. We washed out clothes in a tub with a scrub board. But those things were not too important, because no one else had them either. We learned to live with what we had. We raised our vegetables in a garden near our home. We shared our bedroom with at least one other sibling, because there wasn't space for each of us to have a room. The neighborhood had a house that was converted into a school. That is where the teacher held class with all the students until their twelfth birthday. Then the student was sent across the island to a secondary school. We used to have to walk the five miles each way, until the Army brought in some rickety old buses that we could use. We had a good family life full of values learned from our parents. And we seldom thought about how our life would be without both our parents. My friend's father was killed while fishing. All the other families around that family provided for its needs. The men would make repairs to the home. The mother found some work at the military cafeteria, so that the family had some money. The children picked up the household work that the mother used to do. In fact, we would all go over one afternoon after school and help with the cleaning and washing of clothes. That is as close as I ever came to knowing someone who had no mother and father living with them."

The recorded music wafted through the bar. It was classic Glenn Miller and his big band sound. When he heard some soft strains, Skip said, "Would you like to dance?" They picked a spot close to their table and moved together to the rhythm of the music. They were as close to an embrace as they had been, and it made Skip feel good all over. He felt another erection coming on and tried to divert his thoughts.

"You are aroused, aren't you?" Nance whispered into his ear. "Would you like to go upstairs for a while? You did tell me that you have a room here, didn't you?"

"I would like that very much." Skip did not know what else to say. This lovely lady was reading his mind. They didn't even bother to pick up their belongings as she followed him across the bar and up the staircase leading to the second floor rooms. As he closed and locked the door to his apartment, she drew the curtains back so that the ocean breezes blew into the room.

"I'll be right back," she said heading for the bathroom. When she came out, she was wearing only her cover-up, having taken her swimsuit off. There was an electrifying feeling between this couple. They were hurrying toward what they wanted to have happen. Skip embraced Nance and their mouths found one another. They fell back toward the bed and lit part on and part off with Skip on the bottom. As she felt his turgid manliness, she wiggled herself to further excite him. Their tongues had found one another and were darting in and out in a fantasy. "Take your swim trunks off," she breathed into his ear. "Hurry! I can't stand the wait."

Skip couldn't think of anything appropriate to say. He sat up and stripped off his trunks. As he turned back toward her, he realized that her cover-up was completely open down the front. She lay back on the bed, waiting for him.

They were so excited that the foreplay was quickly over. There was no need for further arousal for either of them. Nance helped Skip enter her and the rhythm of their bodies quickly increased its tempo. They exploded in their joint climax with a feeling that could almost be heard. Then they collapsed into a state of semi-consciousness reflecting the exhilaration that each was feeling. Still embraced, they fell asleep.

Nance looked at the bedside clock. It was two hours later. She rolled over and kissed Skip's cheek. "Hey, big boy. I hope you won't think poorly of me for rushing us up here. I had a feeling that we both needed that. Believe me, this is the first time I've ever even thought of sex on a first date."

"You have been reading my mind all afternoon, until now. Never would I think poorly of you. What happened was as though you knew what I needed. That there was a loving feeling just added to the therapeutic values. Is it too soon to say, I'm in love?"

"It probably is, but I understand what you are saying, Skip. The chemistry between us is electrifying. There is so much more than the words or deeds." She stretched involuntarily along side him. "It is only three o'clock, but I am hungry. Let's get dressed and go out for a bite. Are you game for that?"

"You bet I am. Maybe something light for now. Then lets plan on dining together later at some lovely beachside café. I'll go down and get our stuff out of the bar while you are showering. Then I'll get freshened up, too. I remember from my sister that it always took her longer to get dressed."

When he returned to his room with their towels and personal belongings, Skip could hear Nance singing in the shower. He immediately felt himself becoming aroused again. This woman really did turn him on. He stripped off his swim trunks and stepped into the shower, kissing the back of her neck. Then he snuggled up behind her wet soapy body and let her feel his manhood against her buttocks. She wriggled around to further arouse him, and then turned, putting her arms up around his shoulders and burying her face in his neck. She nibbled at his neck and face, playfully, as he fondled her breasts. They were full and ripe beyond what would have been expected for such a lithe little nymph. They were locked in an embrace while she turned the shower off and drew the curtain back.

Neither of them thought about drying off. They felt their way to the bed and collapsed upon it. Skip lay back and let Nance ride on top of him. And ride she did. If they had a rodeo in Guam, she could have excelled in the bucking bronco competition. Up and down, pumping him for all she could, controlling him so that his penis did not lose its guidance in her. Slowly building up her rhythm, Nance could feel Skip squirm beneath her. She was in control. Just when she thought he could stand no more, she slowed down and let him regain his composure, then started to increase her tempo again. Finally, she could feel her orgasm coming and she stroked her pelvis as quickly as she could. Once again they came together, frozen in time and space.

She lay her head down on his chest and they were speechless for several minutes. "Now, let's see. Where were we," she exclaimed. "Oh yes, I remember. I was taking this shower, officer, when I was suddenly attacked from behind. And it felt so good."

Skip roared in laughter. "Get off me, you little nymphomaniac. It sure is hard to get a shower around here."

"Maybe if you would stop getting so hard, getting a shower wouldn't be so hard either. Anyway, I think I need another shower. Want to join me again?" As they stood there soaping one another, each of them hoped this was real. Their washcloths in hand, they took turns exploring each other's body and loved what they felt and saw.

It was 1615 when they left the room and walked over to Kaulakaua Boulevard. They stopped at the first diner they saw and ordered two hamburgers, French fries and colas. They found a table outside along the walkway where they could watch the people go by, knowing that they were the envy of each single man or woman who strolled along this main street of Waikiki. They were ravenous and hardly uttered a word until their burgers were devoured.

"I'm scared," blurted Nance. "I've never felt this way before. I'm afraid that this is not real—is not happening."

"Well, be assured little lady," Skip said in his lowest bass voice with an effected Texan drawl, "This is real and I aim to keep it that way." Lapsing back into his regular baritone, he went on, "Seriously, Nance, I have been sitting here thinking the same thoughts. In fact, I started wondering if this were real way back there on the beach when you first spoke to me. I can't remember when I've had an experience of a beautiful woman speaking to me first. I mean in a social engagement. And when you gave me that rubdown and agreed to join me for drinks, I was afraid to wake up. And when you encouraged my urges to go to my room, I just knew that it was all too perfect. I have pinched myself so many times I am sure I will have an extra bruise tomorrow. But I decided that even if this isn't real, it is all I have and I am loving it while I have it.

"It is real, Skip. I'm only scared because I have never felt about anyone like I feel about you. Even though we know only a little about one another, I feel closer to you than I have ever felt to anyone else. I had a serious engagement before I left Guam, with an Army aviator stationed there. I was, I thought, madly in love with him, until I found out that he was playing with my mind and my body. For six months we were together, but I know more about you than I ever knew about him. I was glad to be rid of him when I finally figured out he had no intentions to carry through with the engagement, and only saw me as a companion while he was on Guam."

"Please know, dear lady, that I would never do that. Believe me, I am as startled by our day together as you are. I find myself thinking about marriage and that long-term relationship with you. I've never had those feelings rise above my childhood dreams before. And yet I know that we have just met one another."

They strolled along Kaulakaua Boulevard at a leisurely pace. Hand in hand, they looked in each window and entered several shops where Nance looked at clothes or jewelry that had caught her attention. Several hours passed before they came to the junction where the boulevard was almost touching the ocean near where the water's shoreline curved toward the south and pointed at Diamond Head several miles in the distance.

"I have heard the food is great at the Outrigger Canoe Club just down the street," Skip observed. "Let's go sit in the bar until our appetites reappear. They make a terrific drink with rum and fruit juices that they call a Mai Tai. Does that sound good to you, Nance?"

Answering affirmatively, they continued arm in arm toward the famous old club where the locals kept their outrigger canoes during the week, and from which they sailed on weekends, and sometimes during the week when the summer sun stayed above the horizon later. Most of these canoe paddlers were plantation workers who could not get away during the week.

As they entered the Club, they found it to be bursting with noise and full of people. "Commander Emerson and guest, please," he told the young lady at the entrance. "We would like a table in the bar, near the ocean. And we would like dinner reservations for as late as you can make them to still give us time for a leisurely, sumptuous dinner. What has brought this crowd in so early?"

"Right this way, Commander." The lady led them through the side door into the bar area and found them a table with a gorgeous view of the Pacific. The late afternoon sun was playing on the waves and gave the ocean a shimmering golden look as it overlay the natural azure coloring. "We have had our semi-annual awards presentation for canoeing this afternoon. Most of the plantation owners bring their crews in for the occasion. The presentations are done, but the bar is always a mad house for the rest of the day when this happens. It is too late to go back to the fields, and too early to go home."

They each ordered a Mai Tai and sat holding hands as they watched the golden orb sink toward the ocean. The menu for hors d'oeuvres was offered, but neither was interested in food right then. Satiated by the burgers and fries, they wanted to save their appetites for some 'real food' late in the evening. They had consumed three rounds before the sun sizzled into the water and the after glow was replaced by a heaven full of stars.

The crowd that still remained had become even more boisterous than when they arrived. One local made a comment about Nance's origin. "Hey sister, you Wahine?" Another from the same table said, "What you Kin doing with that Haole?" He was referring to what the locals called the white-skinned Americans, and asking what a local girl was doing with a mainlander.

Skip ignored the first comment, but Nance could feel him tense up. She whispered into his ear to just ignore the comment. When the second comment was made, he stood up and addressed the table from which the comments came. "Listen, you wise guys. This lady is with me. She is here as my guest. I will not tolerate any further comments directed toward us."

"Screw you." He heard the voice come across the table. "If you don't like us, leave. This is our place and we don't like you anyway. You mainlanders come over here to protect your interests in our land and then you think you own us. That's shit, man!" Skip thought the wall was moving until he realized that the voice was connected to this huge local who was raising out of his chair as he spoke.

"Skip, please sit down," cried Nance. "Don't get this started. These guys will bury you. Let's just go."

"Not on your life," Skip responded. "You stay right where you are and I'll take care of this." Emerson knew from prior experience, that his best strategy was to pick the biggest guy and attack. The others would assume he was going to be creamed and would not join in. If he could strike first, he might get lucky. He shoved the table right over into the face of the brute who was still in the act of standing. Then Skip came over the top of the table and lunged at the beast. He got in the first combination, a jab to the gut of the big guy followed by a cross to his right eye. Both punches landed as he had hoped, but the big man just stood there and didn't even blink. Skip stepped back knowing that he was in trouble. God knows what might have happened, but he heard two shrill whistles as the Shore Patrol came running into the room. The bear of a man was just about to lunge toward him, when he sidestepped and tripped over the leg of one of the local's buddies. He crashed to the floor and was narrowly missed by the huge mass of man falling forward.

It was over as quickly as it started. The giant hit his head on the edge of the table as he went down. Blood gushed out of his scalp wound, looking more serious than Skip thought it probably was. By now, the Shore Patrol were able to take control and everyone was moved away from the floor area where the hulk was holding his head.

Nance, seeing that Skip was O.K. said, "I am a Navy nurse. Let me see how serious that head injury is." She took a clean napkin off an adjacent table and wiped the forehead of the injured giant. She could see that it was not serious. She said to his friends, "You had better take him over to the clinic to have that looked at and cleaned up. I don't think it is too bad, but they need to cut back the hair line and sterilize the area."

"Are any of you, besides this nurse, military personnel?" The Lieutenant who seemed to be in charge of the Shore Patrol unit was addressing the crowd, but looking directly at Skip.

"I am." Skip answered. "Let's talk about what happened here." After several minutes of intense conversation, the Shore Patrol unit thanked everyone and left.

"Boy that was lucky," he said to Nance. The manager told the S.P. that the locals started the problem, so there will not be any report filed. Not that I would have done anything differently. Thank you for not getting involved, Nance. And I think it was super that you took a look at Goliath before he left."

Yes, well we need to talk about what happened. You just scared the dickens out of me. Do you do this often? Those guys were baiting you, and you fell right into their trap. I tried to warn you. Five more minutes and we wouldn't be talking here. You would be on your way to Tripler or the local morgue. Those guys carry big knives, you know."

Skip could see her tremble. "Are you all right?"

"I just had a flash back to a time on Guam when my fiancé got baited by some locals in a bar. I was their target of derision, but he was their real target. By the time that fight was stopped, my fiancé had twenty-seven stitches taken across his arm and chest where he had been slashed. He spent five days in the infirmary. Skip, I don't want that happening to you. I couldn't stand thinking I had caused it."

"But you just said it right. You didn't cause anything. Those guys on Guam and these guys on Hawaii were looking for a fight and you were just the way to get to me. You are right, though. I do have a temper when I've had a few drinks. Believe me, it never happens while I am on duty or at sea. But I don't want you to see that side of me and I pledge to try to control my temper." He put his arms around Nance and hugged her to him. Her trembling subsided over the next few minutes.

The manager and her assistant came in and cleaned up the mess and extended the apologies of the Outrigger Canoe Club to their Naval officer guests. They were especially appreciative of Nance attending to the head of the big local, whom they called 'Charlie' and whom they said would not be allowed back for a month for his bad manners. The manager asked if Skip and Nance were ready for dinner. They followed her to their table, set among the ferns with an incredible view of the surf playing in the lights that were shining down from the outside of the Club.

After appetizers of longusta, the lobster cousin that inhabits the islands, and endive salad, accompanied be a cold crisp chardonnay wine, the main course was Duck ala Orange served flambeau with chilled champagne. The duck was crisp just like Skip preferred it. Nance had not eaten duck since she left Guam, but agreed that this was like nothing she had ever had before. Served with rice pilaf and dark green asparagus, the dinner was indeed the sumptuous treat they had hoped for. They topped dinner off with cherries jubilee and Courvoisier cognac. Skip explained that his sister was quite a chef and had taught him a few things about cooking. He hadn't tried to do anything since he got out of the Academy, but promised to put together a feast for Nance one day soon.

They were shocked when Skip called for the bill and were told, by the manager, that there was no bill. This was 'on the house' to thank them for staying after the altercation and not letting it upset them and their remembrances of the Club. They thanked the manager and went with her to the kitchen to thank the chef. They promised to return soon, and Skip vowed never again to cause an outburst about which he felt even more guilty now.

As they walked out into the balmy night air and headed back toward the beach walkway, Skip inquired, "What are your hours, Nance? Can you stay with me? We have so much to learn about one another."

"Oh, I don't want this to stop either, Skip. I have to report in for my shift at 0700 tomorrow morning. I would need to catch a bus at 0530 to get the transfers from Waikiki to the hospital on time."

"Not a problem, pretty lady. I have a jeep at the Royal Hawaiian. Stay the night and I will drop you off at Tripler. I have a 1030 meeting at Hickam, but I want to go to my ship before then. The timing works out great for me. We could leave by 0630 and still get you to the hospital on time. Do you need to stop by your place for a uniform first?"

"No. We wear gowns at the hospital, so most of us don't wear uniforms very often. Just when the brass are coming for inspections or to meetings away from work shift. Okay then, it's off to your place for more merriment, is it?"

"Oh God. I can hardly wait." Skip was only half kidding, as he put his arm around her waist and they walked along through the overhanging eucalyptus trees that lined the walkway along the beach. It was still early, at nine o'clock, and they would stop for a night cap at the Royal Hawaiian bar, where this had all begun not more than eight hours prior.

CHAPTER EIGHT

As Skip Emerson and Curt Thomas entered the General's Conference Room at the Base Commander's headquarters building, they were struck with its spaciousness. Submariners valued space. With so much equipment squeezed into so little space on board, they were awed at others disregard for space. Just driving through Hickam Base was an example. If you were walking from place to place, you would consume your entire day doing so. Everyone there was used to the large, open, flat space needed to allow the huge cargo planes to take off and land, so everything was spread out accordingly. The offices at ComSubPac were nicely appointed, but compressed. Here at Hickam, the appointments were no better but everything was expanded. The table to which they were invited looked like you could play football on it, and the room in which it was placed was twice as large as the table.

Each position at the table had a place card. The Air Force (AAF) was represented by a Colonel and Major; Commander In Chief, Pacific Fleet (CinCPac) was represented by a Navy Captain and Commander; Naval Carrier Air Group (CAG) was represented by two Commanders; and Commander Submarine Forces Pacific (ComSubPac) was represented by Captain Brannigan, Commander Fleming, and the two submarine officers. Microphones and recording machines were placed on the table and a court stenographer was sitting ready to record. Emerson decided it was just one step short of a congressional hearing.

As host of the meeting, Colonel Jennings convened the meeting and thanked the attendees for being there. Welcoming the group to General Waring's headquarters, he reminded them that the number of sorties was increasing daily as the need for aircraft in Europe was diminishing and air groups were being diverted to the Pacific theatre. Also adding to the numbers were the bombers who could now use the re-occupied islands as fueling points and could join the Naval carrier-based aviators in attacks on the Japanese fortresses.

He then turned the meeting over to Captain Brannigan who started by summarizing the methods of recovery for aviators who had to ditch their aircraft at sea. He discussed at length the communications between those Naval agencies at the table and their contingencies at sea, whether surface ships or submarines. The flight controllers for the air groups were responsible for reporting an aviator in the sea. That was done by coded radio transmission from the base or carrier back to the command in Pearl Harbor. Then the command would transmit the distress signal out to designated surface ships and submarines that were supposed to be operating in the vicinity.

That meant it would be several hours before any word of a downed aviator got to the fleet for action. In the meantime, the man in the water was subject to drowning in bad weather, capture by the enemy who might also be operating in the area, or being attacked by sharks.

The surface ships could be reached by radio at any time. Such was not true for the submarines. While submerged, they could not receive or transmit signals. Furthermore, the standard operating procedure for submarines called for no radio transmissions from them while they were in enemy waters; therefore, ComSubPac never knew whether their transmissions were being received.

Captain Brannigan reminded everyone of a further complication when the number of persons involved in any communications increased. He cited the old telephone game. In the same manner, there was evidence that coding and decoding of messages and the multiple parties handling them, was causing some confusion and losing some of the specificity of the original distress call.

"We believe," Brannigan went on, "that it is imperative that the distress calls be directed to and received by our ships in the areas. We propose that radios with air frequencies be installed on all ships so the distress messages can be heard directly. We further propose that those designated surface ships and submarines have a person monitoring the emergency frequencies. That will cut out the air controller, the coder, the radio transmission sender, the receiver, the decoder, and the command unit sender. At least six people who took time and inadvertently garbled the information would be eliminated. We will need radios for both the Naval and Army Air Force frequencies, and believe that all would benefit if those emergency frequencies could be standardized.

There was a buzz of side conversations around the table. Colonel Jennings called for a ten-minute break. He correctly perceived that the representatives needed to digest what had happened before the meeting could go on effectively. He called the meeting back to order in exactly ten minutes.

Colonel Jennings summarized the issues before them. "Is there general agreement on the problem outlined by Captain Brannigan? If so, can the Navy and Army Air Force agree to use the same distress frequencies? And how do we get radio equipment to the fleet?"

He turned to the chalkboard where one of his aides had written the three statements. "What do you have to say about the problem, first?" There was quick agreement that aviators were being lost at sea and that Captain Brannigan had pretty well summed up the reasons for many of the losses.

The colonel then focused on the issue of common radio frequencies for distress calls. It was clear the Army and Navy had established those frequencies separately never considering the other military forces at the time they were established. The engineering people agreed that this was not an engineering or technical problem. It was a command decision. If someone in the War Department, speaking for both the Navy and Army, designated a common distress frequency (or frequencies in case the enemy jammed a frequency), that would be accepted by both military arms. Colonel Jennings said this needed the immediate attention of the three flag officers being represented at the meeting. He felt that with the three in agreement, it would be taken to the War Department in Washington for resolution.

The issue of radio equipment was the last of the stated issues. The engineers for both the Army Air Force and Navy agreed that transmissions were either AM or the newer FM frequencies. While FM resulted in communications that were clearer voice grade messages, the transmission distance was limited to the 'line of sight' and could not be heard if a ship was over the horizon. AM signals bent; FM signals did not. If the frequencies were designated within the AM range, every ship and submarine already had equipment on board that could be set to those frequencies.

"That problem," stated Commander Bent of CinCPac, "is that the radio equipment on board our ships is needed for monitoring designated frequencies. I believe that the issue is not a technical one, that is AM versus FM. The problem is one of supply. In order for our ships to monitor another frequency, they will need another radio set as well as another person to do the monitoring."

"I have a question for one of the SubPac people," inserted Commander Nelson, also a CinCPac rep. "How are you going to monitor distress signals when your submarines are underwater? We all know how difficult it is to get a message to a sub which only sticks its radio antenna up once a day to copy messages."

"I will answer that," responded Fred Fleming. "The gentlemen who are with us from one of our submarines are working with our engineering staff on the design of a floating antenna. We have a prototype ready for trials now. The idea is that the submarine could stay submerged and play out an antenna that would float on the surface, but be small enough to be undetected by enemy ships or aircraft. It is about the size of a hose whip, but much longer. We must be able to disconnect the floating whip at any time should a surface contact become aware of the antenna, so it will be expendable and we will need to carry several on each of the submarines that are on lifeguard duty."

"Good question, Commander," said Colonel Jennings taking control of the meeting once again. "Are there any further questions? Hearing none, does anyone disagree with the following agenda: the four senior representatives of the respective services will make an immediate request to their flag officers to resolve the issue of the common distress frequency to be a set of AM frequencies with some latitude to allow for problems of jamming.

"CinCPac will work with ComSubPac to determine how many radios would be needed. We would expect that you will resolve the issue of priorities within your military force, just as we expect that the engineering problem of the communications with a submarine will be resolved.

"The four senior staff reps will stay in contact daily and any person around this table can call this meeting back to order if these issues are not being resolved within 30 days from today. We are adjourned, gentlemen. Thank you for being here."

The ComSubPac contingent met outside the headquarters building after the meeting. Brannigan said, "How do you think it went over?"

"I certainly think that you got their attention," responded Skip Emerson. "I am concerned over the amount of time it can take for these interagency decisions to be made. We need help in doing the job right, and we need it now."

"You let me worry about that, Skip. I agree with you and I'm sure Admiral Pennington will agree, also. I intend to stand on any shoulders that appear to be pushing against us or slowing the process. How are we coming along with the floating antenna?"

"I left a brief report on your desk this morning," said Fred Fleming, "detailing our progress to date and the problems that we are focusing on. The release mechanism is key both to underwater deployment of the antenna and to getting rid of it when we need to. Emerson, Thomas and their crew have been a delight to work with. We got the Shop Super's attention yesterday afternoon when he realized that you and the Admiral would be looking over his shoulder on this one. Thomas and I are going to hightail it over to the shop right now to see if the engineers and technicians have figured out how to make a release mechanism work."

Lieutenant Thomas chimed in, "Boy, I sure do hope that the decision is an simple as was outlined in that meeting, regarding the use of assigned AM frequencies. In fact, since the aviators need us, why not just adopt our current emergency frequencies?"

"Good practical solution, Thomas." Captain Brannigan knew that the fleet personnel would always come up with the most practical answers if you could find the right questions to ask. "I'll make sure that the admiral includes that as a comment in his communications with Washington and the other three flag officers here in Hawaii. That would sure save a lot of time in implementing a solution if we didn't have to change the fleet's distress frequencies. Actually, I think we have the most challenging task ahead of us. If we can solve how to communicate with a submerged submarine, we will have solved a problem that we have grappled with as long as I can remember."

Brannigan drove off toward ComSubPac headquarters. Curt Thomas said he'd hitch a ride with Fred Fleming since they were both due for the same meeting. Skip said he'd drop by after he took care of some paper work waiting for him on the boat. He followed them out the Hickam front gate, turning left toward Pearl Harbor. He drove around to the Sub Base entrance on Kamehameha Highway, while Fred turned off at the main military entrance to Pearl Harbor Base. Skip decided that they were probably going to stop by the supply depot on their way to the Sub Base Electronics Shop where the model antenna was set up.

As he parked the jeep near BOQ, Skip paused to reflect on what was happening. He took a deep breath and, for the first time that he could remember in a long time, savored the beauty of the Hawaiian Islands. In its sweet, fresh smell was the residual odor of Nance. She was with him in all his thoughts. Even through the seriousness of the meeting that morning he found himself thinking of Nance. What would she be doing at the hospital? Would it be better if she were at the Base clinic? Skip had never felt this way before. Could he be falling in love?

He stopped at the laundry next to BOQ first. He dropped off his uniforms and picked up those that were ready for him. Then he proceeded to his room where he left most of his uniforms. He decided to take one with him to the submarine. As he stepped aboard, there were the usual messages awaiting him. Information on the status of repairs that were underway, fleet movements, SubPac daily memos. The OOD briefed him on the work currently taking place topside.

Hearing 'conditions normal' he stepped down the forward torpedo room hatch ladder. Chief Torpedoman Bill Edwards was in the forward torpedo room working on loading some new Mark 14s. Skip stopped to inquire how things were going. Chief Edwards was never one to mince words. "Those Washington jockeys are still given us crap. They tell us the new exploders work, but there's little evidence of change. We took each one apart up at the shop to see what was different. Most were identical to the old ones that don't function magnetically. We sorted out more than forty units to find these that are a different exploder mechanism. I won't be satisfied till we have fired a few."

Skip reassured the Chief that SubPac was putting a lot of pressure on the War Department to get the problem fixed. He did not tell the Chief that he, too, was concerned as to whether the 'fix' was the right one.

After hanging his uniform in his stateroom and grabbing a cup of coffee from the Wardroom, he headed aft as a walk through to see what the crew was up to, and to let them know that he cared about what they were doing. The Control Room was quiet at the time. The Radio Shack was a mess, but the men must be topside working on the installation of the floating whip. He would go up there after his walk through.

The cooks were loading provisions into the freezer located below the mess hall deck. Skip asked if they had gotten what they ordered. Farley Worth, the Lieutenant Junior Grade who was the commissary officer as well as the junior gunnery officer, said that the supply depot had been good to them. They had gotten everything they had ordered in provisions, and a new ice cream machine was being installed later that day.

As he walked through the After Battery compartment, which was bunk space at this level above the battery cells, he stopped to chat with the medic. Doc Ellis, Hospital Corpsman First Class, was the Snook's only medical person. He had a locker in which he stored his medical supplies, except that morphine or other narcotics were kept in the Ward Room locker. "I went to a fascinating seminar yesterday, Captain. They showed us how to perform an appendectomy at sea. I hope that I get a chance to do one of those."

"With all due respect for you abilities, Doc, I hope we don't have the need. I'd rather see you doing that operation here at the clinic or in a hospital."

"But they wouldn't let me do it here. It is only at sea in an emergency that the Navy will empower me to act as a medical doctor. On the shore, I am at best a technician. If the doctors think they are so much better, why don't they ride along with us?"

"They would just get in the way," Skip responded. "You and I know that. They would just be dead weight most of the time on board." Skip thought, but didn't say, that he was always concerned that even the enlisted medics were excused from operational assignment of duties so that they could study and be available for an emergency at any time.

Both engine rooms looked like a tornado had come through. Keeping one engine always on the ready, the other three were torn down and being rebuilt. In addition, the Forward Engine Room reported that the distillers that provided the pure water for filling the batteries when water was lost from evaporation were being thoroughly purged and cleaned out as soon as the engines were overhauled.

In the Maneuvering Room, the electricians were cleaning and burnishing the contacts on the huge levers in the caged area where no one was allowed while they were underway. These levers and contacts were what drove the submarine, switching the power from the generators that drove the motors on the surface, to the batteries that provided the electricity for those same motors while underwater.

Finally, Skip ducked through the bulkhead hatch into the After Torpedo Room. Like a miniature of the Forward Torpedo Room, but without the escape hatch and compartment that hung in the center of the FTR, it was quiet. The torpedomen always worked together so these men were up topside for the loading, just as the forward torpedomen would be topside when they were loading aft. In each case, the men responsible for the respective torpedo rooms would be below deck in the room for the loading procedures.

Skip climbed up the ladder and onto the aft deck. He could see the activity in the sail area where the radiomen were working with the sub base shop personnel. He spotted Curt Thomas over on the pier talking with the crane operator who was lifting something over to the area on the sail where all the men were. Saluting the ensign flapping in the slight breeze on the stern, Skip crossed the stern gangplank and walked over to where Curt was.

"How's it going, Curt? What are you up to this morning?"

"We are putting a box on the fairing, Captain. It looks like we might have a fix on the floater. Hap Henry, our Radioman First Class, thinks he can tie the electrical connections without having another cable from the radio shack. We are installing a splitter box so the cable coming to our whip antenna will split off and also go to the floating antenna."

"This is good news. I always worry whenever we have to cut another hole through the pressure hull. Every one of those fittings provides another point of rupture if we get depth charges close to us. And sometimes, just the sea pressure will pop a gland nut and cause major water problems around all that electrical equipment we have in the Conning Tower. Keep up the good news, Curt. I'll see you below after while."

Back in the Captain's Stateroom, Skip read through the messages and determined that there was nothing he needed to respond to. He initialed the clipboard and placed it on the Wardroom table. He went back into his stateroom with a fresh cup of coffee.

A sharp knock at his doorway brought Skip out of the deep thoughts that had consumed him. "Speak," he said.

"Sir, you have a phone call in the Control Room. A Miss Nance Jones from Tripler Hospital is calling." The duty petty Officer had taken the call and came to find the Captain.

"Thank you," he said. He arose from his desk, stepped into the hallway and strode the twenty steps aft to the Control Room bulkhead. As he ducked through the hatch, he saw the telephone instrument that the electricians ran from the dockside down through the Conning Tower and placed on the gyrocompass glass top in the Control Room.

Skip picked up the handset. "Hello, Nance. This is Skip."

"Skip, I will be getting off at two-thirty this afternoon. You had mentioned that your schedule might allow you to pick me up. How do things look for you?"

"I'll be there. Everything is going well on board, and I'm looking forward to seeing you. I'll come up to the Radiology Department at 1430. Have you had lunch yet?"

"No, I never seem to get a break while on duty. How about you?"

"Me neither. Let's plan to have a late lunch. I know a great Chinese café not too far from where you are and on the way to downtown. See ya." Skip hung up the phone and realized how excited he was just at the thought of seeing Nance.

It was 1345 and Skip knew that it was only a 15-minute drive over to the hospital. He read the logs for the past two days they had been in port and made a couple of changes to the patrol report which he then left for the yeoman to type in final form for his signature. He would need to take the report up to ComSubPac tomorrow by noon to meet the deadline. He stopped topside to talk briefly with Curt to let him know that he could be reached at the Royal Hawaiian later that afternoon. Curt assured Skip that he would stay with the crew on this vital installation and dockside trial. The real trial could not take place until next week when they would go out to sea to check out all their systems. Skip then dashed up the dock, jumped into the jeep, and headed off the base.

CHAPTER NINE

Skip arrived at the second floor where Nance worked at 1425. Nancy introduced Lieutenant Commander Emerson to her colleagues, the doctors and nurses who ran the radiology unit. They all seemed pleased to meet on of the warriors that they served. Skip's enthusiasm for the war and what was happening to beat the enemy back toward his own shores was exciting for them to hear. Usually they only saw the patients who were in no condition to be excited about anything. One of the doctors remarked at how fortunate the Navy was that the attack that so crippled the battleship fleet had left the submarines unscathed. Skip elaborated to him and the others about how that fateful day had changed the role of submarine warfare forever. Previously thought of as support ships to protect convoys, they now roamed the seas independently and were on the attack more often than serving as guards.

Nance came up to the group and announced that she was off duty. "Anyone care to join me for the afternoon?" she said with a cute little quirk in her voice.

Skip did not have to be reminded of why he was there. It was enjoyable talking with these medical personnel about his love for the submarines, but they were a distant second when it cam to the real reason for his having come to Tripler. He grabbed Nance's hand and off they went.

They drove down the hillside enjoying the beauty of the day. The breezes sweeping off the coast up the hillside blunted the heat of the midday Hawaii. With the open jeep, a speed of more than 15 miles per hour was all that was needed to keep the air circulating. When they reached Kam, as the locals called Kamehameha Highway, Skip turned left and headed toward Honolulu.

The Chinese café that he had promised sat on the right side of the road just before they got into the city limits of Honolulu. Quan's was best known among the older natives who kept it busy most nights and every weekend. During the week, however, lunch was an easy time to find a table. Skip and Nance were sufficiently past lunchtime that they weren't sure what Quan would be willing to serve them. Quan suggested the Chop Suey and shrimp dish that he was so well known for. Usually he would not prepare it early in the day, but he knew Commander Emerson from the many times he frequented the café and so he was willing to offer his best to impress his friend and his friend's new guest.

As they sipped their green tea and waited for the chef's work of art, they found it easy to pick up on their conversation from the morning ride when Skip had dropped Nance at the hospital. Skip asked how her day had gone. "Three surgeries required some x-rays. Other than that, there were two radiation treatment sessions and record updates. And a meeting with the hospital chief of staff at 1030 took 45 minutes out of the day, and put us all behind. It seems that there is going to be another reorganization of the military medical system. Some congressional aides are urging the War Department to centralize the medical personnel separately from the three military divisions: Army, Navy and Marines. They would create a whole new medical force. Who knows where that will end up."

"Well we had a great meeting with the Air Force and surface Navy unit commanders this morning. The bought our idea for distress communications and are hard at work this very minute on how to get Washington authority and move ahead. My crew is installing some equipment for sea trials. My XO is doing a terrific job on this assignment. I am really lucky to have him or I would be back there with the crew right now, instead of taking the afternoon off to enjoy your company."

"I haven't met Curt Thomas yet but I already like him. But enough of the Navy. What shall we do with our afternoon?"

Skip said, "I know of this great beach on the other side of Diamond

Head. Out near the blowhole, if you know where that is, is a washed out crater called Hanauma Bay. The beach is good and the water is crystal clear. We can pick up some swim fins and goggles at the Navy sports unit at the Royal Hawaiian and head out there if you wish."

"Sounds like fun to me. I haven't seen the blowhole either. Maybe we could stop be there. Will we change at your apartment or at the beach?"

"We might as well change at my place. We need to pick up our stuff there anyway." Their food arrived and was served by the chef. Skip wondered why they were getting such a royal treatment, but wasn't willing to break the spell by asking.

The food was every bit as good as he had ever had. It helped that neither of them had any breakfast and it was getting late in the afternoon for lunch. They enjoyed the local shrimp that was just caught that morning and had just come in with a shipment for the evening's trade. The fried rice was a specialty of the house and unlike any that either of them had tasted before. Quan responded to their query by saying that he used some cumin in the recipe, and thanked them for noticing the subtle difference it made to the rice dish.

They finished and Skip gave Quan a large tip along with the payment of the bill. This was a thank you for the special treatment, and Skip knew that it would also ensure him of continued special treatment the next time he came to Quan's.

They parked the jeep next to the Royal Hawaiian and went in through the front lobby. Both of them remarked at the elegance of the hotel and shook their heads to think that the government was so willing to underwrite the modernization of the building in return for controlling it during these war years. It was a gamble for the owners, but with tourist trade blunted by the war, it was not much of a gamble.

They picked up the swim fins and goggles, and the new tubes that the staff called snorkels. They went on to the room where they had left such a mess that morning when they left hurriedly, having slept till the last minute. They were pleasantly surprised to find it immaculately clean and their clothes all folded and hung up. Wow! They'd like to get used to this kind of treatment. Skip walked down the hall to where he saw the cleaning staff working on another room. He thanked them for cleaning up the mess, and gave each of the ladies a dollar bill. They smiled and said it was their pleasure to serve the fighting warriors who saved their land.

When Skip walked back into his room, he found Nance awaiting him under the covers of the bed. She beckoned him to join her. Skip stripped off his uniform and underwear, and tore back the covers. There she was in all her splendor awaiting him, looking like the centerfold of one of those provocative magazines. She took him in her arms and pulled him on top of her. Their mouths found one another, and their hands were working frenziedly at each other's erogenous areas. He caressed her breasts that were spread out on either side of his chest. She held him in her hand and stroked him slowly. As their tongues intertwined, she helped him find his way into her. He began moving and Nance moved against him, setting a rhythm that was like a melody of enchantment. Skip tried to control the overwhelming urge he felt, but could not contain himself and came with a physical explosion that almost drove him back out of her. She assured him that they had come together, and he felt better knowing that.

"Well, are you sure you want to go to the beach?"

"Yeh, come on Nance," he said, rolling over onto his side and running his hands over her slender body. "The day is early and there is plenty of time for more of this later. Besides, I probably couldn't perform well again for at least another fifteen minutes." They both laughed at that.

"Last one in the shower has to get the towels." Nance exclaimed at the unfairness as Skip was jumping out of bed even as he said the words. He decided to let her win and headed for the bureau in which the extra towels were kept. As she jumped under the shower, he laid out an extra set of towels for them to take with them. Then he joined her.

Later, Skip drove past the turn-off for Hanauma Bay and drove the mile further to the roadside stop above the famous blowhole. As they stood and watched the phenomenon, Nance asked Skip if he knew what caused the water to come spurting up in the air after the howl that sounded like a giant down there somewhere.

Skip explained that as the waves came ashore, a natural tube had been created and the water pressure running into what was shaped like a funnel caused the air to be compressed. This is what made the howl. As

64

the water behind the compressed air entered the narrower part of the tube caused the vertical spouting.

Nance was impressed. It no longer seemed a mystery once it was explained. Maybe, she thought, some things are best left to be a mystery.

They got back into the jeep and Skip turned it around and headed back to the turn-off to Hanauma Bay. As they drove through the mangroves, they caught sight of the bay itself. Nance's breath was taken away. They were up on the rim of what had been, many years before, a volcano. With the far side washed away, over who knows how many years, the ocean entered. It was about a 150 foot drop from the rim down to the beach on the near side of the bay. They parked the jeep and grabbed their gear for the hike down the path to the beach.

Finding only a handful of people there at the bay, they picked a spot near a cluster of palm trees where they could seek shade if they wanted that later, and spread out their blanket on the sandy beach. Without saying a word, each raced the other to see who could get to the water first. Nance screamed in delight as she hit the surf and stumbled into the water. Skip was right beside her, a step behind. He was not faking it, this gal was fast on her feet. He reached out to steady her and they both fell into the water. Fortunately, the surf here had just come over the coral reef and was subdued. It would not do to have another episode like the one on Waikiki Beach that had precipitated their meeting. They got to their feet and Skip took Nance's hand as they walked forward into the deepening water. All about them they could see the teaming sea life. Beautiful striped fish were nibbling at the hairs on Skip's legs. Nance laughed at the sight. Then she dove into the water and he followed. When they came up in a few yards, Nance said, "Let's get the goggles and fins, and see if we can make those mouth tubes work. I've never seen anything like this before. Even the aquariums look dull by comparison."

They walked up out of the water, got their gear, and returned to the surf where they sat down in the water and pulled on the fins. Donning the goggles, they stuck the curved part of the tubes into their mouths and headed back out into the water. They swam and dove in the shallows along the shore side of the coral reef for the next half hour. "I've had enough for now," Nance said as she came up for air and saw Skip also on the surface. "I'm going back to the beach. Stay as long as you like."

Skip stayed out in the water another 15 minutes. When he got back to the blanket he told Nance about playing 'hide and seek' with a baby octopus who would peek around the side of a rock or piece of coral till it saw him, and then would go darting off to the next one.

"It's hard to believe that there is a war going on out there," Skip said to Nance. "When I am here with you in this idyllic setting, it is easy to forget what brought us here. I have lived for the sea since my senior year at the Naval Academy. Now I find myself looking for opportunities to get away from my ship and be with you. I know that I must go back to sea soon, and I frankly dread it because it will take me away from you."

"I share your thoughts, Skip. But we must realize that we took commissions to help our country in this war. You as a warrior. Me as a medical specialist. We must accept that we will be separated because of our roles. That doesn't mean we won't miss one another. I feel about you in a way that I have never felt about anyone else. But we must be strong in our resolve that we will cherish our time together and look forward to the day when this is over and we can always be together."

"Thanks, Nance, I needed that. I think that I was starting to feel sorry for myself. I guess that I am jealous of those doctors at the hospital who will be with you while I am away."

"But they are professional colleagues, not lovers. Many of them have a loved one on the mainland who they miss just the same way. People that they won't get to see even occasionally until this war is all over. We are the fortunate ones. We have one another and we will get to see each other when your sub is in port. Let's focus on that as happiness. I will be here waiting for you each time you are at sea. And when you are here, we can have these interludes in our life. I can't think of anyone with whom I would trade places."

As the sun settled below the rim of the western side of the old volcano, Skip and Nance gathered their things and headed up the walkway to the parking area. They got into the jeep and headed back toward Waikiki. Their moods were somewhat pensive. Skip knew that they wouldn't have many days left before his submarine would be ordered out to sea. He loved his ship and crew, but he would miss Nance terribly.

These past few days had brought him a happiness that he had never known existed. He found himself wanting to clutch onto time. It was a strange feeling.

They decided to go back to the Royal Hawaiian for a shower, change of clothes and a drink while they decided where to dine that evening. They barely made it to the room before Skip was all over Nance, smothering her with kisses and his hot embrace. They did not make it to the shower until 35 minutes later.

Sitting at their table enjoying a Mai Tai and the view of the sunset, they were both much more relaxed now, and the glow of a loving couple exuded from them. The bartender and anyone else in the room could see the aura around them. They sat next to one another, as was their custom at a table. Sitting across the table would have inhibited their touching. This way they could hold hands or lean over to kiss each other.

"I know a place called the Palms, not more than a mile from here. A pond teaming with Koi surrounds the dining area. The seafood selection is varied, depending on what the fishing boats bring in for that day, but everything is good. And the trade winds rustling through the palm trees give a whispering effect to the ambiance. The Tiki torches light the paths that lead from the entrance to the thatched hut dining areas."

"That sounds terrific. Lead the way."

After an enjoyable dinner in the delightful setting, they returned to the Royal Hawaiian. Parking the car in the lot, they decided to kick their shoes off and walk in the sand along the Waikiki shoreline. The sand was still warm and the ocean revealed its glassy surface. This was one of those infrequent nights when there were no waves beating up on the beach. They headed up toward the park end of the beach walking slowly arm in arm.

"Somehow, I cannot imagine being back in Iowa. I've become accustomed to the beach, the sun, and being able to find a great restaurant or drive a short distance for a change of scenery. Back home, the towns are small and the amenities are few. On a summer night, we would swelter in the humidity that often matched the temperatures, and would drive out to the lake to go fishing, only to be eaten alive by mosquitoes. Maybe we should think about staying here after the war. Could you settle for paradise?"

"Anywhere with you is where I want to be, Skip. Being raised in a village on Guam, we had no amenities. We had the beach and could catch as many of the local fish as we could eat. But the beaches weren't as pristine as these are. No one cleaned those beaches daily and they were strewn with whatever the high tide left behind as it ebbed. Poor people don't see the same things we have come to know. Fallen palm trees are left to rot. Roads are graded once every five years whether they need it or not. Thatched roof huts are not just a place you go for a wonderful meal. They are what we all lived in. Sharing a single room with a half dozen siblings and having no running water and a toilet out back, we too yearned for a better way. That is why my parents have instilled the need for an education in each of their children, so that we could get away and know another life. Fort Dodge, Iowa may have only had three movie theatres with movies that were two years old by the time they got there, but on Guam, the only movies were shown on the military bases, and the locals were not invited."

"It is all a point of perspective, isn't it?" Skip appreciated the gentle reminder that maybe he had not been so bad off as he thought. No matter how bad you thought things were, there was always someone who could tell you from personal experience that things could be worse.

At the park end of the beach, Nance showed Skip some stretching exercises that didn't take equipment or a lot of room, and Nance thought Skip could learn them and use them while he was on the submarine. It felt good to stretch out the muscles. As they warmed up, Skip could smell that special smell of Nance that he would always carry with him when they were apart.

They ran back along the beach till they reached the area in front of their hotel. There they sat on the sand to cool down. Skip kissed Nance, and the embrace reminded him how much he loved her. "Do you want to go out to a night club?"

"How about if you get us a bottle of wine and we stay right here tonight?" responded Nance. "This spot in the sandy beach is where I'd prefer to spend this evening."

Skip said he'd be right back, and headed up across the grass to the hotel bar. He was back in a couple of minutes with the wine, an ice bucket, two glasses and a tablecloth. They sat there talking, embracing, and enjoying their wine as they looked toward the star studded heavens.

Skip pointed out the constellations to Nance. She knew Orion's Belt and the North Star that, at this latitude, was almost on the horizon. Skip's old navigator skills returned to him, as he pointed out groups of stars that she had never heard of. In each case, they paused long enough to envision the constellation being described. Skip then told Nance how the navigators of ships had used the star positions for thousands of years to set their courses at sea. He was at his professional best when he was comfortable with his subject matter.

When the wine was gone, they gathered up the bottle and glasses in the tablecloth and set it on the closest outside bar table, and headed for their room. Covered with the residual sand from their laying on the beach, they stopped at the beachside shower and rinsed themselves off. Then they headed around the side of the hotel to the entrance closest to their room. The peeled off their swim suits and jumped into the shower to get the sand out of places they couldn't very well expose at the outdoor shower.

"That sand gets into every crack and cranny," Nance said as she was busy with a washcloth flushing out the sand. "Here. Let me help you." She soaped up the cloth and started at Skip's shoulders working her way downward. As she got to his loins, he suddenly had an erection as she touched him. She laughed, but refused to stop her rubbing. As she squatted there beside him, they forgot what they were doing and were caught up in this foreplay. What followed involved each of them exploring the other's cavities as they had never done before, and ended with a sexual climax they would long remember. They lay on the floor of the shower enjoying the wet warmth of the water pouring down on them.

The alarm woke them at 0530. Skip reached over and turned it off, and Nance reminded him that it was a working day and she was due at the hospital at 0730. Neither remembered getting out of the shower, or into bed, but there they were. Skip started the coffee while Nance got first bid on the bathroom. He slipped into a robe and walked out onto the deck of the apartment. The early morning view of Diamond Head was spectacular with the sun's rays just touching the highest point of the

Head. The breezes of the night had subsided and the air was already growing warm. He heard the shower starting and went back inside to join Nance there.

He dropped Nance at Tripler and headed for Pearl Harbor. It was still early enough that he decided to have a leisurely breakfast on board. The sub base was still pretty quiet as he drove through and parked at the head of the finger pier where the U.S.S. Snook was tied.

CHAPTER TEN

Hap Henry was raised on a farm just outside of Madison, Wisconsin. He had an interest in radio back to his early childhood. His mother and father had a radio in the living room that they listened to. He saved his money and purchased a crystal set when he was eleven years old. He strung the wire antenna out his second floor bedroom window over to the top of the barn, some 75 yards upwind from the house. In the evenings, he would try to find programs that he liked. That was the start of his career in radio electronics. And it was the remembrance of that antenna that made him suggest the idea of a floating whip antenna.

Once the electronics designers had figured out how to store and deploy the floating whip, the next step was to try it out. The U.S.S. Snook had become the beta test site and every day for the past week had been the site of a half dozen engineers working around the shears installing and testing the antenna. They were ready for sea trials now.

"Let's plan on going out at 1300 hours. Have your radioman send a message up to SubPac that we are testing 'Operation Lifeguard' on fox radio at 1430 hours. Can we pull enough of the crew back to run this submarine?"

"We will have about 55 men on board anyway, Skip. We could go operational with that many, heaven forbid that we should have to."

The XO passed the word through the public address system that they would get underway for local sea trials at 1300. You could sense the sudden quickening pace of the crew in getting their tasks done and everything tied down in preparation for the day. Thomas asked that two base engineers join them for the afternoon to see first hand how their project was going to work, and to be on hand for any fixes that were needed.

They backed out from the pier and headed out the channel promptly at 1300. By 1330 they were clear of the channel and into open ocean. They turned to starboard and headed for Barbers Point. After a test dive to set their ballast, they were ready for any operational orders. Only then could they concentrate on the radio antenna.

They dove to 65 feet. Captain Emerson manned the large periscope and the XO was on the attack scope. Each wanted to see the antenna deployment firsthand.

"Give the order to release the floating whip," said Emerson.

"Radio, this is the XO. Release the floating whip."

"Aye, aye, sir," responded Hap Henry. He pushed the electronic plunger that had been located on the wall of the radio shack. The lid on the antenna case would be released and the whip would float to the surface if all went well. The sub's motion forward would cause the deployment out behind them.

"I see it. It's starting to play out behind us now. Do you see it, XO?"

"Yes sir. It is operating exactly as we planned. Any forward movement of the boat will let it deploy behind us on the surface. Do you mind if I go below to watch Hap Henry receive on the antenna?"

"Go below. Pipe the radio into the Conning Tower so I can hear too."

Curt Thomas quickly climbed down the ladder into the Control Room and headed into the Radio Shack located in the after corner. Hap Henry had already shifted the antenna control from the regular whip antenna to the floating whip. He was setting the frequencies for copying the standard fox radio transmissions that were on almost all the time. Thomas joined Farrell, Henry, and the two base engineers in crossing their fingers that the antenna would work.

The immediate beep of the coded message told them all was well. The message was as clear as it would have been through the vertical whip antenna. The XO challenged Henry to make sure that he was, in fact, switched to the floating antenna before calling up to the Skipper about their success. He asked if they could increase speed from the two knots they were presently doing to the maximum of eight knots for underwater. The Captain called for increases in speed at three-minute intervals until they were doing eight knots and the floating whip was streaming out behind them like a fishing line. Each of the base engineers was given a chance to observe the antenna through a periscope. Hap Henry got to take a look also. They were all overjoyed with their success. They tried turns and backing down to see what would happen. Physically the lightweight antenna stayed with them. Electronically it did not make any difference to the signal strength.

The final test called for detachment. It was agreed, however, that the floating whip needed to be retrieved for examination and any further testing at the base shop. They slowed to one knot before Hap Henry hit the detachment plunger. The Captain had turned his periscope over to one of the base engineers who joined the XO in watching the antenna.

As soon as they could verify its success, the Captain called for surfacing the sub and recovery of the antenna. Within 30 minutes it was gathered up and they were underway again for Pearl Harbor. The next test of this antenna would be a real one somewhere off the coast of Japan.

Jim Farrell asked the Captain if he might test the engines after their overhauls, on the way back into port. Emerson turned control over to Farrell with instructions to call him to the bridge when they had entered the harbor. He went below to enjoy a cup of coffee. The Snook commenced a high speed run back towards the channel entrance, testing each of the engines in sequence and then adding engines until all four were providing full power to the propulsion motors.

Skip Emerson stopped by the Radio Shack as he came down into the Control Room. The base engineers were examining the antenna inch by inch. He asked if everything was O.K. They told him that there were a few technical adjustments they wanted to make, but that they would certainly consider this a successful test. Skip asked Curt to prepare a report on the testing for him to review before he left the boat that afternoon. It was important that they get a report in the hands of ComSubPac before the next meeting of the joint powers on this project.

Skip knew that the base engineers would lose no time in contacting Commander Fleming, their boss, but wanted Captain Brannigan and the Admiral to have first hand acknowledgement from the operational fleet. Skip decided that he would take the report draft up to Brannigan this afternoon.

CHAPTER ELEVEN

P hil Brannigan had agreed to stay at his office until Skip Emerson could bring the report by. The verbal indication was very positive. Brannigan smiled to himself. He had picked the right team to get this done post haste. Emerson was a proven leader, and he had done a good job of keeping his nose clean. Thomas had turned out to be the kind of coming leader he had guessed: thorough and competent, and a team player.

As Emerson and Brannigan sat talking about the project, each man respected the other. Emerson said how much they all appreciated Brannigan going to bat on using the emergency frequencies that the Navy already had in place. Brannigan told Emerson how much he appreciated the speed and precision with which the design, installation and test had taken place. This team had taken 'a big deal' and made it appear as though it were an everyday occurrence. The admiral had pushed the right buttons to get the new radio equipment brought from stateside. It would be in the Supply Center the next morning. Needless to say, the U.S.S. Snook would get the first piece of equipment installed immediately.

"Skip," Brannigan said, "How would you like to show your innovative spirit in another way? We are looking for a leader like you to head a group of boats operating together in a manner somewhat similar to the German Wolfpacks that were so effective in the Atlantic. Are you ready to go on a group war patrol to test out our theories?"

"I'm sure we could, Captain. We are practically ready now. This floating whip was all that was holding us up, and it appears to be ready for a real test. While most of us are skeptical about the Wolfpack concept, I guess that we will never really know how good or bad it is until we try it out."

Skip Emerson left ComSubPac headquarters with mixed feelings. The Navy had been talking about the Wolfpack concept for several months. As they sat around the Officers Club talking, the submarine skippers had voiced their concerns. They would be giving up some of their freedom to command, because one of the three subs would be placed in command and would carry a Wolfpack Commander, a senior officer who would otherwise be going to squadron status. They would be expected to communicate with one another when history had shown them the best transmission was no transmission. On the positive side, however, they could 'herd' some ships toward one another and that should increase their kill ratio from their independent searching. Most often, they used their surface speed to get into position with enemy ships. That meant moving at night when they could not be seen. In the daytime, their speed underwater was so restricted that they seldom got into position for a torpedo firing. How would these positives and negatives work out? Only time would tell.

Skip and Nance had agreed to meet at her apartment that afternoon as soon as he could get there. He called the hospital on his way up to see Captain Brannigan, but she had left already. He called the apartment, but she had not arrived yet. Oh well, she would expect him to get there when he could. She probably had called Pearl to see if the sub had come back in from operations that day.

She knew that sometimes these things got out of control and an afternoon test run could turn into several days. Besides, he had been in port two weeks now, and she knew he would be going out on patrol soon. As much as she dreaded that day, she knew it was part of his life and was not part of their life together.

She showered and lay down to take a nap. When she heard the knock on her apartment door, she glanced at the clock on the bedside table and realized that she had been asleep for almost two hours. "Yes, who is it?"

"'Tis I," came the voice she knew to be Skip's. She opened the door and gave him a sleepy-eyed smile. He hugged her and followed her into her bedroom.

"What shall we do with our evening, Miss?"

"Where shall I start? How about staying right here? You could tell me about your day at sea. And I am sure that we could find something to do."

"Looks like we are going out next week. Frankly, I have mixed feelings about that. I've never felt this way before, Nance. I love the sea. It is my home. I have always looked forward to the patrols. Now, since we met, I find that I want to be with you. I know that my training and experience is needed at sea, but my heart says 'don't go' and I am frustrated about all this. We need to give this new antenna system a real test and if we can save some aviators, that would be a real plus. But I would rather be with you."

"And I would rather be with you. But that must wait, Skip. You and I would never have met if it weren't for the war. We must remember that our duty to our county comes first. Even when our hearts tell us otherwise, we must be strong in our attention to duty. Let us pledge that after this is all over, we will then acknowledge our true feeling for one another and decide where that will take us. Let's just live one day at a time for now."

Skip kissed her. "You are an incredible woman, Nance. You have said in a very few words what I needed to hear to reinforce my feelings. What a gift you have. Was your Dad a preacher on Guam? Or did you pick that ability up somewhere else?"

"Actually, I think I owe it to my Mother. She was always reminding us kids of our greater reason for being." Then she laughed, "But let's don't get too serious about all this. The night is young. And I want us to enjoy this day before we plan the next one."

CHAPTER TWELVE

A ll back, one-third. Cast off all lines." Captain Emerson was in control from the bridge of the U.S.S. Snook as they backed out of the pier at the Submarine Base. "Port ahead two-thirds. Right full rudder." He waved to the pier where Nance had joined a few of the base personnel to give them a send-off. "All ahead two-thirds. Rudder amidships." They were underway for another war patrol, this time as part of Wolfpack One including the U.S.S. Sargo and U.S.S. Stingray, both of which were preceding the Snook up the channel. The Sargo had been named as the Unit Command ship. Emerson was glad it was not Snook because the Unit Commander, CDR Steve Gallagher was on that boat and the ship's captain would be relegated in his command. At least Snook and Stingray enjoyed some autonomy that was no longer present on Sargo.

It was a balmy 80 degrees already at 0800. This was going to be a scorcher in Honolulu, but they could feel the breezes blowing off the ocean and knew that they should enjoy these remaining hours of sun. Where they were going, there would not be much surface time during the daylight, and the weather was often fogged over at this time of the year.

They were loaded down with a full compliment of torpedoes and provisions for a six-week patrol even though they only expected to be gone four weeks. They could always off load any unneeded provisions on their return at Wake or Midway where the Naval personnel were not normally treated to the special provisions of submarine food. And the full load of torpedoes had to be rationed to make it last for four weeks, let alone a longer period. The Washington War Department brass still felt that only one torpedo should be fired at a merchant ship. The submarine skippers knew that they would miss half of their targets if they did not fire a spread of torpedoes.

With their trim dive completed and ballast tanks set for the heavy load, they were ready for any action. The three boats were escorted until sunset, so that they could make 21 knots on the surface. At the last rays of sunset, their escorts turned back for Pearl Harbor and the Wolfpack proceeded with their patrol orders.

They would run at high speed during the night unless they saw a target. They would stay submerged during the daylight hours unless fog coverage was sufficient to let them run on the surface. The Sargo would dictate their surface running and therefore their progress toward the designated area of patrol. Once again, the pack needed to stay together, something that the individual submarine commanders abhorred.

Midway was to be their first stop, to top off fuel. The subs would go into port one at a time in case of enemy attack. The fact that Midway had not been attacked for more than fourteen months meant nothing to the Naval planners. Precautions were still the order of the day.

So, one by one they went into the fuel pier, topped off, and returned to the waiting area for the other two boats.

When this maneuver was completed, they once again headed for their target area in the East China Sea, west of Okinawa. It would take five days of steady transit to be on station in time. That was the mission of Commander Gallagher and no one doubted that they would get there when they were supposed to. Even if it meant passing up an opportunity to sink an enemy ship, these old timers were more into the strict letter of their orders that the younger sub commanders who knew what their mission was supposed to be. The Navy had realized this flaw in leadership the prior year and had set about replacing most of the more senior shippers because it had become apparent that the risk takers were the more successful captains. Now with the Wolfpack scheme, there was a need for a senior commander to direct the efforts of a group of sub skippers. And many feared that we were going backwards in our leadership style.

On every patrol, the Captain was expected to command the boat while they were at General Quarters. Since most of the action took place during the night hours that meant shifting the biological clock so that the Captain slept during the daylight hours and was awake during the night hours. It wasn't always that clear cut, but the idea stemmed from the fact that they stayed submerged during most daylight hours and ran to positions of attack using the cover of darkness. Of course, if they sighted a ship that they could overtake during the daylight, they did so. Others found that their primary duties took place while the ship was not in action and, therefore, got their work done during the day while the boat was submerged.

The engineering officer was one of those assignments that required attention around the clock. His engines and batteries provided the propulsion; the hydraulic and high pressure air systems determined the submersion; and the pumps and motors performed all the functions needed to operate the submarine. These pieces of machinery needed repair that was done, for the most part, during those quiet days. But his crew was essential to the attack mode, running engines and switching the propulsion in the Maneuvering Room. The critical task of charging the batteries could only be done when the boat was on the surface so that the engines could run the generators.

Lieutenant James Farrell felt like he never got caught up on his sleep. He was always catching a nap when he could. Sometimes he would get five hours of sleep, but not often. Other times he would not get three hours sleep in two days.

It was hard to communicate to all the officers with their varying schedules. The daily log was the responsibility of each watch officer who posted any unusual items. The Captain and XO made daily entries in the logbook about items that were essential to all hands. Other than that, the two senior officers took turns making the rounds of the boat during each watch so that they became aware of any circumstances. The Engineer also posted items of equipment that were out of commission during repair and maintenance periods. That posting was in the Control Room for all to see. Each Watch Officer reviewed the postings before assuming the responsibilities of the watch.

The rest of the crew was divided into three watch sections. Each watch section operated the board for two, four-hour periods a day. That meant each crewmember stood eight hours of watch each day, in addition to performing the maintenance and repair tasks that were expected of him. Many of the crew took their watches in their areas of responsibility, so that there was considerable overlap of the times for operation and maintenance. For instance, the Enginemen stood watch in the engine rooms where they could work on the engines, generators, and distillers that were located there. The Torpedomen stood watch in the torpedo rooms where they could make ready the torpedoes and work on the tubes and auxiliary equipment located in those compartments.

The Electricians were a hybrid. Some of them stood watch in the Maneuvering Room where they were expected to be at the controls to react immediately to any orders for changes in speed or shifting from generator to battery power for the propulsion motors. Others roamed the boat, taking specific gravity of the batteries every hour and checking operational equipment, including the holding tanks for the heads that had to be blown out into the ocean periodically.

During the daytime, the Officer of the Watch, typically serving as the Diving Officer while they were submerged, was responsible for checking on the status of the boat and for maintaining the two planesmen who operated the bow planes for depth control and the stern planes used to maintain a level configuration; and by the Chief of the Watch who stood at the manifold controls watching the light and dial indicators of hull openings, air pressure, compensating weight in tanks, and hydraulic pressure.

The Watch Officer was in charge of the boat until relieved by the Captain or other senior officer. He was expected to know the status of the boat and its equipment, and to report that status whenever one of these senior officers came through the boat to check.

When the sub went into action for any reason, the Captain or Executive Officer would take command of the boat from either the Conning Tower if they were submerged, or the Bridge if they were on the surface. At that point, the Diving Officer's tasks and responsibilities were reduced to those actions emanating from the Control Room. The Captain would decide whether the XO would join him in the Conning Tower for offensive actions, or would stand behind the Diving Officer in defensive or evasive maneuvers.

And so the days went by, especially when they were in transit. Endless days that drifted into one another, broken only by the occasional drills used to test the preparation of the crew to react to some emergency condition, hoping that if a real emergency arose, the crew would know what to do almost automatically.

The days on station were different. Everyone was at the ready, hoping for a ship to wander their way. The men slept fitfully, expecting to hear the sound of General Quarters at any minute. They slept dressed for action. Some of them did not change clothes for days at a time, a source of irritation and discussion by the old timers in the crew's mess during those times when there wasn't anything else to fuss about.

They were under pressure to keep the boat in operating order while on station. Any repairs would be done, while worrying that at any time an order to put the equipment back on line would come. Little problems were logged but not taken care of. These were a source of concern because a little problem left undone often became a big problem before long. A slight bearing vibration noise, often isolated by holding the working end of a screwdriver against the casing of the equipment and placing the ear near the handle end, was bound to become a serious problem when the balls contained in the racing of the bearing inner and outer surfaces finally let go. At that point, there was no decision but to stop the piece of equipment and replace the bearing hoping that no further damage had resulted.

CHAPTER THIRTEEN

Lookouts below," bellowed the Captain, turning his head toward the periscope shears behind him where the port and starboard lookouts stood on their platforms. Even as they were jumping down the hatch into the Conning Tower, the Captain continued the orders, "Dive, Dive," and hit the klaxon switch twice to signal all hands that the submarine was going underwater.

In the engine rooms, the diesels were shut down. The Maneuvering Room switched the power from the engine generators to the batteries while awaiting specific orders for the reduced speed.

The Captain was the last one to clear the Bridge. As he slid down the ladder into the Conning Tower, he held the lanyard that closed the bridge hatch behind him. The Quartermaster climbed up the ladder and dogged the hatch at which time the Captain dropped the lanyard. Seconds later he was sliding down the ladder from the Conning Tower into the Control Room. As he appeared below, the Chief of the Watch said, "Green board, Sir."

"Very well, Chief," the Captain responded knowing that this meant that all the hull openings were secure and the boat was flooding down. "Take her down to 150 feet," he said to the Diving Officer who then gave explicit orders to the bow and stern planesmen and the Chief who was operating the manifolds.

"Blow negative to the mark," the Diving Officer said to the Chief, bringing the submarine into a state of near neutral buoyancy where they could change their depth without further flooding or blowing of water in the tanks surrounding the hull.

"Sonar," the Captain continued, standing behind the Diving Officer, "Keep feeding us ranges and bearings to the Sargo and Stingray so we can plot their movements."

"Aye, aye, Sir," responded the Sonarman from his compartment. "I have them at 400 and 800 yards off the port bow, relative position is 320 degrees."

"Very well," was Emerson's response. "Steer 350 true. Give me Ahead two-thirds." With those orders the Helmsman made his course corrections and rang up two-thirds speed to the Maneuvering Room from which he got a response on the motor annunciators.

The three submarines had dived together at a predetermined time. The Wolfpack One commander wanted to try out some strategies for underwater attack. They had predetermined certain deployment patterns of the three boats before they left Pearl Harbor. This was the first opportunity to try out the maneuvers before they met up with an actual incident.

They were to travel at the predetermined course, speed, and depth for ten minutes before they broke out into a star formation to surround the enemy ship. Sargo, in the lead, would race to get to the far side of the target. Stingray would veer to starboard and move abreast of the target. Snook would linger behind the target. Thirty minutes later, if all went well, they should have the target surrounded and Sargo would signal its position by firing the first torpedo at the target. The torpedoes had been preset for short runs so that if a torpedo missed its target it would not continue to run towards another of the Wolfpack submarines. The torpedoes were also set for running above twenty feet so that an errant torpedo would stay close to the surface and the subs could operate at periscope depth and still be safe.

The plotting team was able to follow the movements of the other two subs from the sonar data. It would be important to know the patterns followed by the other skippers when they got into real combat. True to form, the sonar operator reported a firing of a water slug some 30 minutes later, the Sargo's signal that the test maneuver had been completed. The boats surfaced and continued their run toward the East China Sea.

Skip Emerson and Curt Thomas sat sharing a fresh pot of coffee in the Ward Room as they critiqued the exercise just completed.

"It's not worth it!" exclaimed Thomas. "This Wolfpack crap is just too inhibiting. We have all been trained to trust our judgments and work as independent units. Now we find ourselves part of a team taking orders from someone we barely know who can never see things in a unit the way we see those same things separately."

"I agree Curt. I am very concerned. I fear that the old boys who decided to do this are only focusing on the success of the Germans— another Navy at another time and in another part of the World. I hate the idea of having to wait for someone else to decide what we should do. I intend to stay as independent as I can from the pack. But I don't think we will influence the decision makers until enough sub commanders have tried it, to make a unified and purposeful statement against it. In the meantime, we will comply with the concept but be assured that I will opt for the broadest of interpretations that I can."

"It just isn't fair, Skip. We have drilled our crew for months. We have this new radio gear on board. And now someone else is going to decide how and when we get to try it out. I know that all this grousing isn't going to make any difference, but it does make me feel better getting it off my chest. Just think. At least you commanders of today get to do things on your own. Who knows what we, the next class of sub commanders will be facing. Maybe the Wolfpack idea will expand instead of blowing up. Many of us came to subs because we knew that surface ships were always part of some larger force and never got a chance to exercise their independent skills. That was what made the underwater Navy so unique. We may lose some of out future commanders if this word gets out."

"Well, I am assured that some time during this patrol, Snook will be called upon to take up station for a 'Lifeguard' operation. The bombing flights are getting heavier by the day and that means there will be more allied planes going down. The surface ships can't be everywhere. Even when they try to stay in an assigned area, they get chased out by enemy convoys who are just trying to disrupt the saving of the downed aviators. If we can show that the floating whip antenna works while we stay hidden under water, we will have found a significant new role for submarines in this war."

"The sooner the better. I say," said Thomas speaking for all of them. By the way, Skip, I made the rounds of the boat earlier and Number 1 Distiller was making a lot of noise. I asked Chief Jones to have the enginemen look at it first chance. Everything else seemed to be in good shape after our submerged run."

"Better make a note of that to Farrell. We don't want our Engineer to get his nose out of shape because he wasn't informed of the problem." Skip Emerson reached over and picked up the teapot off the electric hot plate and refilled their cups. "I understand that the last two crew members are ready for their qualifications walk-through before they get their dolphins. Do you remember that experience? To me, it is just like yesterday that I was put through the paces. I guess maybe it is something we each never forget."

"You bet I do. You were the XO that drilled me. I think I had to throw away the khaki trousers I was wearing that day because you made me crawl through the pump room tracing the high-pressure air lines from the pump to the auxiliary tank. I will always remember that. I decided that day to be a little easier on the crew members that I take through qualifications."

"Yeh. Well don't be too easy. I remember that I was not sure how familiar you were with the auxiliary tank. But you sure got familiar that day. You want to be sure you are surrounded by crewmembers that know what is going on in case of an emergency. Having redundancy in back-up systems doesn't mean a thing if your crew can't work those alternate systems in a crisis."

"I hear you, Captain. You are right, too. And our officer colleagues have to know it all if they are going to lead the enlisted crew through those emergencies. Every time I hear about or read about a lost sub, I wonder if it could have been saved. Who knows when some obscure system could have prevented flooding of a compartment, or bypassing of an electrical system or using hand driven pumps when hydraulic power is out could make a life-saving difference."

"Captain to the bridge." The 1MC address system interrupted their discussion, and both men jumped to their feet and headed aft through the Control Room and up the ladders into the Conning Tower and on to the Bridge.

"Captain coming up," called Emerson as he stuck his head through the hatch to the Bridge. "What's up?"

"We have received a light signal from the Sargo that they want up to close up so the Commodore can talk to the three skippers by bullhorn. We are closing now at 1000 feet and I knew you would want to be on the Bridge for this maneuver."

"Very well, Mr. Worth. The XO will take the conn while I am manning the bullhorn. Keep us no closer than 100 feet of their port side, Mr. Thomas." The Captain was always official in his language when they were in the company of enlisted personnel.

"I have the conn. Aye, aye, Captain," responded the XO. "Steady as she goes. Steer 200 degrees on the rudder," he called down to the helmsman who repeated the orders back as confirmation.

The three submarines wallowed in the stage two sea like three whales basking in the moonlight. Sargo was in the center, its Bridge area some twenty feet ahead of the other subs lined up along each of its sides. Stingray was on the starboard side and Snook was on the port side. Each submarine was about 100 feet off the sides of Sargo.

"This is Gallagher talking. Please acknowledge."

"This is Emerson, here." From the far side, Emerson could faintly hear Sam Cook on Stingray responding.

"Our exercise today was good. I think we can make it work. We should be on assigned area by morning. We will dive a t 0615 and maintain 65 feet and periscope depth. Operate according to Wolfpack One Orders Three One One. That is all. Godspeed."

"Come port to 150 degrees, XO," said the Captain. He could see Stingray starting to execute a turn to starboard so that the three boars were moving apart. "Give the conn back to Mr. Worth when you are ready. I'll meet you in the Ward Room for discussion on orders."

"Aye, aye, Sir," responded the XO. "Mr. Worth, you have the conn. Making turns for 18 knots. Steering back toward 200 degrees. Keep your eye on Sargo and Stingray. If they turn or submerge, follow their lead and call below immediately." Curt Thomas headed down the ladder after the Captain. He stopped in the Control Room to talk with the Chief of the Watch who stayed close to the manifolds in case a dive order was called. Then Thomas went forward to join the Captain.

"Big deal," he said. "Now we know which of the operating orders we are to go by. Two bits says it calls for kissing his ass."

""Here they are, Curt. Let's read the orders again to make sure that we clearly understand them. Some of the maneuvers called for might get a little sticky if we 'jig' as the 'jag' out there. The two of them sat and read Op Orders #311 again to make sure they understood them. Each signed and dated the Orders and left them on the table for the other officers to digest. The alternate orders were put in the safe so no one would confuse them with the ones that were placed into effect by the Wolfpack One Commodore.

The area of the East China Sea that they were to prowl would focus on two shipping lanes. At the north end, Shanghai was a major port and ships traveled from there due east to Nagasaki on the island of Kyushu, Japan. At the south end lay Taipei, Formosa. The shipping from there traveled along the islands and atolls that stretched south and west below Kyushu. Now that the allied forces had once again taken Okinawa and several lesser islands in the chain, the ships would leave Taipei and hug the coast of China until they got to Shanghai where they could pick up the shipping lanes to Nagasaki.

Wolfpack One had entered the area above Okinawa and was heading south by southwest to ward Taipei as their first patrol area. Formosa was manufacturing much of the supplies and materials needed by the Imperial Forces for this war. If the submarines could bring that shipping to a halt, Japan could not sustain its offensive. Already, Japan was suffering from the loss of goods and materials from the Philippines and from Okinawa and other major islands where the Japanese armies had robbed and pillaged while they occupied the land.

It was evening and the Snook had been running on the surface with its convoy for about three hours when a starboard lookout spotted lights from a ship on the horizon. The Captain and XO were called to the Bridge to confirm the sighting. The Captain ordered the boat to flank speed and came starboard of the target bearing in accordance with their Wolfpack instructions. They were unable to tell whether their target was one large freighter or two middle sized ones at this range. No escorts could be seen, but they could not be sure there was not some protection hidden over the horizon.

The skipper went below to the Conning Tower to study the target through the periscope. "I see two sets of lights overlapping one another," he called to the Bridge. "Looks like two good size freighters. They are running with navigation lights on that means they don't expect any problems out here. I still cannot see any sign of escorts. Be sure that the lookouts are looking around us so no one can sneak up from the rear. I am going to stay on the scope as we make our approach."

He called down through the Conning Tower hatch to the Diving Officer standing by in the Control Room. "Sound General Quarters. Stand by to dive, but we will continue to run on the surface as long as we can." He hoped that they could get ahead of the freighters so that their slow underwater speed would not cause them to lose their firing position. He asked for a range and bearing from the radar operator, and confirmed that they were moving toward the position they were assigned. The blackness of the surface on this moonless night made it impossible for Emerson to spot the other two submarines but he knew they, too, were heading for their relative positions. Another thirty minutes of flank speed and they would be ready to dive and get into their firing position.

"Captain, this is the Engineering Officer. We have a serious heating problem with Number Two engine, Sir. Can we reduce speed to full?"

"Negative, Mr. Farrell. We need everything we have to get into position. Take a few revs off that engine if you must, but continue to answer bells for 'Flank' on the others. I need at least 21 knots to get there on time.:

"Aye, aye, Sir. We are at 23 knots now. I will make sure we do not get below 21. In fact, I think we can do 22 knots and still relieve the engine heating problem."

With a margin of five minutes, they were on station and ready to dive. Skip Emerson took a look all around with his big lens before lowering it. They were about 2500 yards ahead of the two freighters and to their starboard. This was exactly where they had agreed to be. The Captain called for clearing of the Bridge, then ordered the dive. The Snook slipped quietly under the water and leveled off at 60 feet.

The orders were given to open the outer doors on the Forward Torpedo tubes that had been loaded and prepared as the boat headed toward its current position. Mark 14s were ready in all six tubes that were now flooded down and ready for final settings.

The Sonar Operator heard no change in the screw pattern of the freighters indicating they had noticed anything. He also said there was no noise in the water to indicate the other subs had fired any torpedoes. Sargo was to fire the first ship, but Emerson knew that he could not wait too long or he would lose his position. The seconds went by as though they were hours. There was absolute silence throughout the boat as everyone waited to hear something.

The XO was in the Conning Tower with the Captain. "What do you think, Skip? Are they out there? Why hasn't Sargo fired?"

"I don't know, Curt. But I do know that we cannot wait more that one more minute, or we are going to lose out position.

"Final range and bearing," Emerson said as he moved the cross hairs on the attack periscope directly on the foredeck of the leading freighter. The XO dialed in the solution and set the tubes electrically to fire a spread of four torpedoes starting with the visual bearing and staggered back toward the fantail of the second ship. There was still no noise out there.

"Fire!" called out the Captain. Immediately, the XO hit the plungers to fire the tubes electrically. In the Forward Torpedo Room, the men standing at the tubes duplicated the orders firing the impulses just in case the electrical firing did not function. This procedure was standard, and it made sure that there were no misfires.

"Torpedoes away," responded the Gunnery Officer from the Forward Room. "Tubes are clear and flooded down. Permission to reload the tubes one through four, Sir."

"Permission granted," Emerson turned and called out, "Sonar, what do you have out there?"

"Four torpedoes running hot and straight. No other sounds in the water, Sir." As the Snook's torpedoes headed for the freighters, the other submarines were also firing, but the water noise from one covered the others and each thought it was the only one firing at the time. Each sub would later take credit for sinking the two freighters, but no one would ever know which torpedoes had struck first. What they each saw was a huge series of explosions that marked the end of the freighters. If there were any survivors, it was because they were blown off the deck. The ships were sunk on the spot, with their hulls breaking up from the concussion of perhaps 12 torpedoes.

ComSubPac might later argue whether it was necessary to expend that many torpedoes, but no one could deny that those two ships would no longer be carrying any materials to Japan or any other place. They were rubble on the bottom of the Sea.

Captain Emerson called for surface action to see if there were any survivors, and to rendezvous with Sargo and Stingray if no other ships or aircraft were sighted. The gunnery team would act as the rescue team if any survivors were spotted. That team assembled in the Forward Torpedo Room where they would use the forward hatch if needed topside. In the meantime, the lookouts were doubled up to search the air and the surface. As they surfaced and the Bridge hatch was opened, Captain Emerson was the first one topside. He swiftly searched around with his binoculars before calling the rest of the Bridge detail topside. He could see the other two submarines breaking surface.

"Have the Quartermaster bring up the small light," he called down into the Conning Tower. He had the signal 'V' for victory flashed toward Sargo's position and then toward Stingray. Each responded with 'V' indicating their sentiments. Then the three boats turned towards their prior search pattern and spread into their formation. The Captain called for full speed on three engines and called the Engineering Officer to authorize leaving Number 2 off line so the engine men could determine the overheating problem. Once they had cleared the area, they would settle down to cruising at ten knots and there would be plenty of time to recharge the batteries before dawn. The men had been secured from General Quarters and things had settled back into their routine, if there was such a think for a man-of-war in these enemy waters.

The Engineer caught up with the Captain in the Ward Room two hours later. "Number 2 is all set, Captain," he said. "We found a sea valve that was not opening all the way, so we changed it out. Everything has been tested and is working properly. Thanks for letting us back off the RPMs back there. I fear we would have torn up the engine if it had kept going."

"Good work to find the problem so quickly. I am impressed by you, Jim, and by your engineering gang. You keep this bucket running like it was new."

"Thanks, Captain. I'll pass that along to the men." Farrell headed aft and Skip turned to Curt Thomas.

"What do you think about that run, Curt?"

"I think we could have sunk those two ships by ourselves. Worst case is, we could have waited for Sargo until it was too late to shoot. Best case, there was a duplication of torpedoes fired. I just don't see how this Wolfpack thing is going to work I know that there have been a few times when we would have liked to have someone chase an enemy ship toward us, but I don't see how that is going to happen if we are all in convoy formation like we are now."

"I agree, Curt. We have got to spread out so we can help each other, if this is going to be successful."

CHAPTER FOURTEEN

They steamed along for the entire day to get on station. From that point forward, they were given greater latitude to work as a unit independent of SubPac control. That night Snook, using its light unit mounted on the Bridge, signaled to Sargo its recommendations that the three subs travel further apart in order to drive the enemy shipping toward one another. They were to stay within ten miles of one another, within visual contact by light signal at night. Otherwise, each of them would roam the area looking for enemy shipping. It would not, Emerson realized, be easy to implement, but he welcomed the relief and the freedom to once again be a hunter.

As they closed in on the larger landmasses, Formosa or the China mainland coast, they would find Sampans fishing everywhere. They had to be careful about detection, in case any of the fishing boats might be carrying radio equipment. Hap Henry kept one of his radio receivers tuned to local military channels, but Emerson and his fellow officers weren't sure that other frequencies were not being used.

On a few occasions, they snagged the fishing nets and dragged the fishing boats behind them. They would have to surface that night and cut away the nets. Sometimes the boats that were not willing to lose their nets would be following along. On these occasions, the Gunnery Officer and his men got some target practice with the deck gun trying to sink the fishing boats without killing the fishermen. They did not take any of these civilian fishermen aboard as survivors. Usually there were enough Sampans in the area to pick up the fishermen at dawn.

On a second day of patrolling, a large freighter was seen coming out of Taipei harbor at dusk. Captain Emerson offered Curt Thomas the honor of taking the command in this attack. The XO was excited about the opportunity. He called for General Quarters and, since they were already at periscope depth, called for the After Torpedo Room to prepare all four of its tubes for launch. Sure that the other two subs would cover the harbor entrance from their angles, Thomas brought Snook around into position where he was going to get a three-quarter shot at the bow as the freighter came out. With everything at the ready, he waited patiently as the huge, lumbering freighter cleared the breakwater of the harbor. With some luck, she might sink right there where she would block other ship movements.

"Ready Tubes Seven and Eight," he barked. "Give me final bearing and range. Mark!" He turned to the Captain who was at his side in the Conning Tower and who had set the bearing and range into the Torpedo Data Recorder. "Fire Seven and Eight."

"Torpedoes away," came the voice message from the After Room. "Reloading Seven and Eight."

"Con, this is Sonar. I heard some noise in the water before we fired our torpedoes. I believe Sargo or Stingray got the jump on us. Since they are further away, we will get first chance at the hit, but I will try to monitor their torpedoes. Also, the freighter is making a lot of noise, trying to increase speed and turn away from us."

"Aye, Sonar," responded the XO. "I think we waited long enough that they won't have time to turn."

The crew felt a loud explosion as both the torpedoes found their mark and buried themselves into the forequarters of the ship. Several others that were almost echoes followed this noise. Both Emerson and Thomas knew that these echoes were the torpedoes from their companion boats joining in the sinking of the freighter.

"All ahead full," ordered the XO. Since they were firing with their stern tubes and facing away from the harbor entrance, they could clear the area quickly. As they moved into deeper waters, they could see a group of escort men-of-war coming around the far side of the freighter. These enemy ships would have to squeeze out of the harbor single file, since the huge hulk filled most of the entrance way, but they would be looking for the submarine that caused this mess and would seek the revenge that their senior officers in Taipei would expect from them.

"What does the fathometer show as water under the keel?" The XO waited for the response to be called out of the Control Room. When he heard that there was now 250 feet below them, he ordered, "Take us down to 175 feet and reduce speed to one-third. Rig for silent running."

The XO knew that the enemy ships would not have a sound bearing to follow until they got out into open water. He was not anxious to use their battery capacity until he needed it. For now, he was satisfied to sit quietly and see which direction the enemy took. They might pursue one of the other submarines, hardly expecting that there were more than one out here. Then they could have some real fun.

When they reached 175 feet, the XO called for "All Stop. Secure all motors." They hung there, silently listening to the water noises of the other submarines and the surface craft in pursuit. It was clear that their ploy was working. The Japanese destroyers went right over the top of them and kept on going.

"Bring me up to periscope depth, quietly," he called down to the Diving Officer. As the attack periscope broke the surface, the XO could see the trailing ship about 400 yards directly in front of him. "Prepare to fire Number One. Set for course 000 relative. Fire."

The thrust of the torpedo was the only noise from the submarine. Its high-pitched whine could be heard for the first fifty yards of its voyage. Everyone held their breath as the seconds ticked by. And then they heard 'Kaboom' as the torpedo drove up into the stern of the destroyer that never even knew it was a target. Covered by the noise of the explosion, the XO ordered right full rudder and full speed ahead to get them clear of the area from which they had just fired. As the submarine dived, the last look out the periscope was of a mass of destroyers circling around, now sure that they were headed the wrong way. Thomas got them back down to 175 feet quickly and, once again secured all the noise makers.

About three minutes later, a loud explosion greeted them, approximately two thousand feet off the port side and on the surface. They could only guess until it was confirmed, but hoped one of their

Wolfpack colleagues had used this opportunity to hit the destroyers from another side. This was, Skip and Curt nodded to one another, the real showing of the Wolfpack. Just when they think they are headed toward the underwater devil, it pops up somewhere else. It would be hard to imagine that there were two or more submarines out there. That had never happened before.

The effect was grand. A third explosion followed several minutes later, as the third destroyer was sent to Davey Jones locker. Sonar reported that the remaining destroyers were so confused they were heading for the harbor like dogs with their tails between their legs. The XO asked the Captain for permission to come up to periscope depth for one more look. Emerson granted permission as anxious as Thomas to see what havoc they had caused.

The huge hulk of the freighter was lying on its side in the harbor entrance. Two destroyers were sinking fast and the third as listing so badly that it was doubtful it could make it back into port. The other destroyers were working their way around the freighter's hull to get out of harm's way.

When the crew was settled back into their routines, Captain Emerson called a meeting in the Ward Room and congratulated the XO formally before his fellow officers. He said he intended to detail the patrol report and ask for a special commendation for the Exec.

CHAPTER FIFTEEN

Wolfpack One headed north and west toward the coast of China. They knew there would be no ships moving out of Taipei for several weeks, until the freighter's remains were removed from the harbor entrance and until the shipping lanes were searched to find what was lurking out there.

They spent the next two days and nights without a sighting. Aerial reports out of this region indicated ship movements along the coastline up to Shanghai. The Wolfpack found absolutely no targets in the area except for the fishing boats. They decided these Sampans might have been the basis for the aviators' reports.

As they approached Shanghai, they turned eastward to follow the shipping lanes toward Kyushu. They spotted a flotilla coming out of Shanghai with three huge freighters protected by destroyer escorts all around. It would be two hours until darkness would provide the cover they would need to catch up and get into position. Emerson called for a heading that would lead to an intercept position, and ordered turns for six knots. He knew the batteries would be practically exhausted by the time they could surface and recharge, but this was too good a target to turn away from.

He ran at periscope depth and chanced a look every ten minutes or so to determine whether they were losing too much sea between themselves and the convoy. The zigzag pattern of the ships diminished their speed of 12 knots to about half of that. If he could maintain six knots, Emerson knew his relative position should be maintained. He prayed for some overcast that would let them surface early. He knew that the Japanese surface radar was not very effective, and that chances were slim that they would be detected by radar. But the lookouts on that many ships would not leave much to chance if a visual contact were made. Emerson was even concerned about the wake of the attack scope because the waters were so smooth. He saw some clouds on the horizon and hoped a storm might be heading their way bringing with it a surface chop and some haze.

As he search around, Emerson suddenly saw the Stingray, far behind its intended position, surface so it could catch up. Suddenly, the convoy reacted. The rear escorts pealed off and headed for the sighted submarine. The freighters and the rest of the escorts stopped zigging and headed northeast away from Snook's position. Through his periscope, Emerson could see the size of the wakes increase as the ships increased their speed. He could only hope that Sargo was on the far side and might be able to corral the convoy or head them toward Snook.

AS it turned out, Sargo was not yet in position, needing some time to run on the surface, too. Stingray's premature surfacing had caused them to miss this convoy, and placed them in a position to take on the escorts who were equipped and trained for dealing with submarines. Hopefully, the three boats could provide a surprise the surface destroyers had not contemplated.

Emerson called for General Quarters and ordered all the tubes loaded with Mark 14 steam torpedoes forward and electric fish aft. The steam torpedoes were set for short range and maximum speed of 45 knots. The electric fish were slower, but much more accurate and could home on the surface ships' hulls. They turned toward the destroyers that were speeding toward the position of Stingray even as that boat dived.

Captain Emerson took bearing and ranges until he was within range of the leading destroyer that was cutting across his bow some 1500 yards distant. Setting the proper speed and projected course into the TDR, he called for firing of two torpedoes from the Forward Torpedo Room complement with a sufficient spread to pick up at least one of the overlapping hulls.

A thundering explosion caused Emerson to peek out the periscope and revealed they had hit the stern of the leading ship where the crew had just been loading the depth charge racks. The explosion was intensified as the flash of the hull explosion set off the depth charges. The entire rear of the destroyer was gone and it started to sink fast. The other three destroyers were confused. They could not figure out which way to go. It was impossible for their target submarine to have moved to this new position so quickly. The two leading destroyers held their course and the lagging destroyer turned toward Snook.

"Take her deep, all ahead full, steer right full rudder," Emerson ordered in quick succession. "Go to 200 feet and report back." The well-trained crew all knew what was expected of them and each one did his job with little further communication. They leveled off at 200 feet on a new course of 060 true at eight knots, and reported to the Captain. "Very well. All stop. Rudder amidships. Rig for silent running. All ahead one-third. Give me a reading on the battery."

The Diving Officer responded. "We have about 15 minutes of battery left at one-third speed. We have shut down all equipment including the air conditioning motors. We can sit in one spot for up to two hours on our remaining battery."

"Sonar reports an explosion off in the distance, Sir." The XO was at the Captain's side listening to Sonar reports. "We hope that means Sargo got a shot at the convoy." The crew could hear the pounding of depth charges nearby and some of those in the distance that must have been targeting Stingray.

And then, as suddenly as it had started, all became quiet as the noises from the destroyers were reported as fading into the distance. Assured that they had at least delayed the submarine or submarines, the escorts were hurrying back to the convoy to protect the freighters who were under attack from some other submarine. They left behind them any chance of survivors being picked up from their sunken comrade.

"Score one man-of-war," declared Captain Emerson. "Well done, men. We will stay at G.Q. while I take a look topside. We will sit still until we can surface and get a charge going on those depleted batteries. Dinner will be served 15 minutes after surfacing. All hands should know that we will head for the convoy while we charge our batteries. We are not yet finished with this enemy. We still want those freighters sunk. That is all."

An appreciative response was heard throughout the boat as the men reacted to their Captain's message.

Once the area was determined to be clear, Emerson ordered the diving officer to surface the submarine and they immediately began to charge the batteries. A full and complete charge might take four hours, but Emerson doubted they would have that long before they were in the thick of battle once more. From the Bridge, he ordered ahead full speed on two engines that were not engaged in the battery charge. With this quiet sea, they could probably attain 17 knots. Captain Emerson knew that the other two submarines must also be in need of a battery charge. If it took longer to catch up with the convoy, so be it. They would not be able to attack unless they had the battery capacity to sustain an underwater attack and perhaps a longer evasive period.

Plot gave him the bearings of the convoy and they headed in the direction that would cause their interception in three hours. Sunrise would not take place for another six hours so they had plenty of time to maneuver under cover of darkness. And they knew that the convoy could not get sea support in that amount of time. Air support would come as soon as sunrise afforded a visual target from the aircraft. As he thought about it, the battery charge became even more essential to their mission.

Emerson searched around for Sargo or Stingray but could see nothing. A slight haze was a welcome addition on this night. The XO asked permission to come to the Bridge, and came up to join Emerson.

"Do you think we can get the batteries charged before we pull the plug, Skip?

"I think that we have to, XO. We want to avoid a surface attack if we can. We may have to do some evasive procedures. And sure as we stand here, there will be aircraft over us as soon as the sun rises. We may be submerged for a long time."

"We can't let this convoy get away from us. Are you sure we cannot go after them on the surface? Our gunnery team have been doing a lot of drilling getting ready for their chance."

"I don't think a submarine stands a chance of surface battle against a destroyer. Those ships are made for fighting on the surface. They have ten times more armament and fighting guns than we do. Submarines are designed to work with stealth under water. We need that advantage to be effective. Surface action against the Sampans or even patrol boats is one thing; against larger men-of-war, we will always be on the short end of the stick. I don't think any amount of preparation can change that advantage.

"In fact, I have recommended to SubPac that the guns should be taken off our decks. As we get more action in shallow waters and are entering harbors where there are extensive minefields, several skippers have agreed that we should remove all protrusions that could snare a mine. We are even studying putting sheet metal around the periscope shears to protect us in this area above the Bridge. Submarines need to be smooth and sleek if we are going to be effective in areas of mine fields. You should also be aware that we may be able to penetrate those mine fields soon with a mine detector that is being tried out at Pearl."

"Just know, Skip, that we stand ready to take on the enemy with our topside guns if you need to call for such action. I marvel at your ability to stand here in the face of battle and talk about what may be in the future. Most of us are secretly hoping there will be a future as we see how close those destroyers come with their depth charges."

"You can change 'most of us' to 'all of us' if you want," Skip replied. "I think we all harbor some anxiety every time we go into battle. But that doesn't stop us, does it? Our superior training gives us the edge for success at what we do. No surface ship crews are as carefully selected as ours. We can count on each of our crewmembers to do what is expected. Those surface ship commanders probably have more than half of their crew who are new or just don't know what they are doing."

The radar reports showed that they were gaining on the convoy at a speed difference that should put them into position within two more hours. As he glanced at his watch, Skip Emerson realized he and Curt Thomas had been talking there on the Bridge for 45 minutes. The Captain asked the XO to take the Conn so he could go below for some relief and a walk through the boat. Emerson wanted to see and hear first hand that his crew was ready for additional sustained action.

After stopping at the head, and grabbing a cup of coffee, he stepped into the Forward Torpedo Room. Bill Edwards, the Chief Torpedoman in charge of both torpedo rooms, was talking with his men up near the tubes. He greeted the Captain and told him what they were doing to prepare the torpedoes in the racks for quick loading into the tubes. Emerson noted the cleanliness of the room. Bill Edwards was a quality person who believed that people worked as they lived. And this was, after all, where the torpedomen who ran the Forward Torpedo Room lived. The only time they left was to go to the mess hall or to take a shower. They were self-contained otherwise. The Sonar men took up the rear part of the compartment, located near the external sound heads that fed them information. Emerson gave them a 'thumbs up' indication, not wanting to interrupt their constant listening for any noises beyond their own.

Emerson then headed aft through the Forward Battery compartment where the Ward Room and staterooms for the officers and chiefs were located. He then entered the Control Room where all the activity was centered when they were underwater. While they were on the surface, there was an eerie quiet. Only the Chief of the Watch was stationed at the manifolds location. Since they were at General Quarters, the Diving Officer and two planesmen were standing by for any orders to take the boat down.

He stopped by the Radio Shack as he headed toward the After Battery compartment. The two radio operators were listening to Fox Radio and copying any orders of interest to any submarines, so Captain Emerson and his officers would get any general information about ship movements.

The Mess Hall was practically empty. The Cook was preparing some pastries for the crew, one of the night specialties on Snook, and greeted the Captain as he stuck his head into the small cramped galley. "Everything O.K. Cookie?"

"Sure thing, Captain. We got all da men fed an back to their battle stations in record time. I'm fixin' extra supply of dem sweet rolls ta have on hand. Look like we at GQ for long time."

"Good thinking," responded Emerson. "An effective submarine rides on the stomachs of its crew. You are doing a great job of keeping our men healthy and ready, Cookie."

As he entered the crew's sleeping area, he stopped for a short visit with the Hospital Corpsman who served as medical specialist on board. These guys were enlisted petty officers who would be technicians on a Naval Base. But our here, they were the only medical people available and were sometimes called upon to operate on injured or sick personnel as though they were doctors. They clearly operated outside the letter of the law, but with the full backing of every submarine commander afloat.

Emerson ducked through the hatchway into the Forward Engine Room where the Chief Engineman was talking with the Engineering Officer and his men. They were busy repairing one of the two distillers that provided precious water, first of all for the batteries, and then for drinking.

One distiller just kept up with the demand for battery water and the Cook's requirements. In these hot climates where evaporation required daily refilling of the battery cells, the electricians could be seen stooping under the deck plates of the two battery compartments for hours at a time, filling the cells from a rubber hose with a filling device that looked like the ones at a gas station, but not metal. Static electricity was a problem that submariners were careful to watch for. No metal was worn when the electricians went into the battery wells.

The second distiller was a backup unit, but its operation let the crew have ample drinking water and some water for the showers. The pumps on these distiller units were a source of constant irritation to the enginemen who repaired them.

After telling these enginemen he was indebted to them for keeping these tired old engines running so well, and having Lt. Farrell join him as he toured the remaining engineering spaces. He repeated the message to the After Engine Room crew, and then stepped through the hatch into the Maneuvering Room that was also a part of the Engineering organization. The giant cage protecting personnel from the high wattage levers and contacts filled the center half of the room. The walkway went to the port side of the hull and back to the area where the two operators stood their watch at a panel of levers and dial indicators. These two men and their Chief Electrician were looking through some records to see when they had last burnished the contacts on the controllers in the cage.

At the same time, they were operating two engines to drive the sub, and charging their batteries with the other two generators.

"How long till we have our charge completed?" asked the Captain.

"We need another 90 minutes to get a decent charge, Sir," responded the Chief. "We should have an hour beyond that to get topped off, but I have a feeling that is not going to happen at this time."

"Give her everything you can, men. I will keep us on the surface as long as possible and will try to give you warning of shutting down the battery charge before I call for dive. I cannot guarantee that, you know."

"Aye, aye, Sir. We know that you do what you can."

The Engineer stayed behind to talk with the electricians as the Captain stepped into the After Torpedo Room. The Torpedoman First Class was in charge of this room while his Chief was up forward, and it was similar to the Forward Room except that it was smaller, had only four tubes, and shared its space with the housing for two giant motors that turned the propulsion screws. After chatting with the crew assembled there, Captain Emerson headed forward to the Control Room.

The Chief of the Watch and Diving Officer were having a heated conversation as he approached them. They were arguing about whether the Brooklyn Dodgers could take the crown away from the Yankees this year. Both were New Yorkers who loved to argue. It seemed to Emerson that baseball was a good subject for them to be arguing about. He went up the ladder into the Conning Tower and, after checking with the Quartermaster on their latest position, went up to the Bridge.

"Everything seems in good shape below. The spirits are high. Other than one of the distillers being out of operation for a while, all the essential equipment is on line. I will take the Conn now, XO."

"Aye, aye, Sir. We are still more than an hour away from being in position. We are traveling at the same course and speed. Radar scans do not indicate any alteration in the convoy heading. Will we be able to get our battery charge in?"

"The electricians want about 80 minutes more," Skip said looking at his watch. "I think we can give it to them. We will need as much battery as we can get today. I think we can slow our speed to 15 knots to make the difference. I don't want us to get on station too soon and then have to wait to go into action. Do you concur with my calculation?"

"I do, Captain. May I lay below? I want to check our plot and fix our position. It's too overcast to shoot the stars tonight, but I know that you will want a confirmation of about where we are before we submerge."

"Right on Mr. Thomas. Lay below."

"Permission to bring radio messages to the Bridge," called Hap Henry up the ladder from the Conning Tower. Receiving permission, he scrambled up the ladder and took a deep breath of the fresh air as he handed the message pad to the Captain. "It feels good up here, Sir. I haven't been topside since we got underway. Calibrating that new equipment has taken any free time I might have had. The XO said I'd better get these up to you if I wanted to breath fresh air for the next day or so."

"Anything serious in this pile?"

"No sir, just standard reports from Pearl, along with some messages from the fleet that we copied. It kind of brings the war up to date. I can leave it on your desk or in the Wardroom if you prefer."

Skip Emerson flipped through all the messages, reading a few of them. He asked Henry to place them in the Wardroom so all the officers could read them. Henry went below.

The Captain scanned around the surface and then talked to the lookouts. "As we get close to that convoy, you need to keep constant vigilance. One or more of the destroyer escorts may move away from the convoy to try to intercept us or the other two submarines out here. Report anything, even though you cannot confirm it. Then I can help you determine whetner there is really something out there. And be prepared to jump down off your perches quickly if I call out to clear the Bridge. We may not get much notice."

Emerson wondered where the other two submarines were. He hoped they were also moving into position. Without any communications, he could only guess that they were finishing their own battery charges and jockeying for position. He also hoped that none of them would be detected, as the Stingray had been last time. Those freighters would look awfully good on Snook's record.

The tension built as the minutes drug on. Several times he heard the call of one or the other lookout only to find nothing. There was more debris in the ocean as they closed in on the convoy. Surface ships had a bad habit of throwing their garbage and trash over the fantail without weighting them down. It became a clear indication that the convoy was ahead of them in the direction from which the waves washed the junk.

Radar reported the mass of ships was less than 15,000 yards off the port bow. If it were not for the overcast, they would have visual contact now.

The Captain called down to secure the battery charge and shut down the two engines providing the charge. When he heard the engines' exhaust quit, he knew they were as ready as they would ever be. And yet he did not want to submerge until they had to. If the could stay on the surface ten more minutes, that would be ten minutes of battery time saved, all other things being equal.

The starboard lookout reported he could smell diesel fumes. Emerson confirmed that heavy exhaust was in the air. They must be getting close and downwind from the convoy or some part of it. He decided it was time to pull the plug.

"Lookouts below," he called out. As they scrambled past him, they reported that they were going below. He was alone on the Bridge. "Dive, dive," he said through the public address system and hit the alarm klaxon twice. He then slid down the ladder to the Conning Tower, grabbing the hatch lanyard on his way. He hung on to the lanyard as the Quartermaster scrambled up the ladder to set the hatch closures.

"Take her down to 65 feet." He turned to the helmsman, "Order two-thirds speed. Steer course 350." He received affirmative responses from both the Diving Officer in the Control Room and the Helmsman still in the Conning Tower.

"Sonar, what do you have out there?"

"Still a lot of noise from us, Sir. But there are multiple screw noises coming from 345 off our port bow. Believe range to be 13,000 yards, Sir."

Emerson ordered the attack scope up and took a quick look all around. Nothing was yet in sight. They were blinded by the haze and would need to use the Sonar for their approach. He lowered the scope and turned to the XO telling him to set the initial bearing and range information for the torpedoes from the Sonar data, and to get reports from both torpedo rooms that they had all tubes ready and flooded down.

He ordered, "All stop." so that Sonar could get a better bearing on the ship noises without having to try to filter out their own noises.

"I hear one of the escorts leaving the convoy and heading away from us, Sir."

"Very well," responded the Captain. He called for the scope while they hovered at 65 feet. Suddenly there was a break in the haze and he could see the silhouette of the convoy. "All ahead, full. Bring the rudder right ten degrees. Hold me at this depth. Make ready tubes One and Two. Permission to open the outer doors. Range and mark to the nearest freighter's mast."

The XO read the indicators into the TDR. "Looks like the crosshairs are on 9000 feet, Sir. But the bearings are closing so their speed will help us close on them. I estimate ten minutes to firing range."

"Conn, Sonar. I hear some depth charges off in the distance. Looks like one of the submarines is being pinned down, Sir. The convoy is speeding up to get away from that area. Believe they are coming at us."

"Hot dawg!" exclaimed the XO. "We have them, Skipper. I'm ready when you are."

"We are going to fire on the leading freighter with Tubes One and Two, then turn and shoot at the following freighter with our stern tubes. Then we are going to high tail it out of here." The Captain had raised the scope and taken bearings every 60 seconds. "Slow to one-third. Steady on the helm. Diving Officer, prepare to take us deep as soon as the stern tubes have been fired."

After what seemed like an eternity to the crew standing by to do their parts in the attack, the Captain called out, "Final range and bearing. Fire when ready."

"Tubes One and Two fired electrically and confirmed, Sir."

"Very well. All ahead full. Right full rudder. Make ready Tubes Nine and Ten.

The sub came around with its stern pointed toward the convoy some 3000 yards distant. As the Captain raise the scope to get range and bearings on the second target, he saw what they all felt as the first two torpedoes hit their mark in a giant explosion.

"Final range and bearing. Fire when ready."

"Fire Nine and Ten mechanically," called the XO through his phones. "Firing confirmed, Captain. Something malfunctioned with the electrical firing control here."

"Take us down to 200 feet quickly. Left full rudder. Steer 245."

"We are at 200 feet, Sir," called out the Diving Officer from below.

"All stop. Steady as you go."

The Helmsman answered, "All stop. Steady on 245, Sir." As the motor enunciators signaled 'all stop' he completed his steering maneuver.

They heard no explosions indicating they had found their target, but knew some of the escorts must be headed their way. Now was the time for their Wolfpack colleagues to take the attack.

The depth charges were scattered over the area where they had been. Fortunately, they enemy still believed that submarines could only go down to 150 feet so they set their depth charges too shallow. Even then, the concussion caused in the water was transmitted with a jarring feeling for half a mile around the point of detonation. Water does not compress, so the explosion causes displacement and with it, the shock wave that can be almost as devastating for nearby targets.

Only one set of depth charges took place, then the destroyer left. Emerson hoped this meant the other Wolfpack members were doing their thing. He called for a slow rise to periscope depth.

The surface was covered with debris and crewmembers in life jackets. They almost speared one sailor as they poked their periscope out of the water. The Captain quickly searched around. They were in the middle of where the convoy had been when the first freighter was hit. That freighter was rolling on its side, just about ready to sink. The second freighter was listing and on fire. Emerson believed that one of the other subs must have made that hit. One of the destroyer escorts was picking up survivors as the others had spread out looking for the enemy. Emerson quickly calculated the angle to that closest destroyer.

"All stop. Hold on this heading. Open the outer doors on Tubes Three and Four. Make ready to fire. Set Depth for six feet.

"Final range and bearing. Fire."

As the two torpedoes sped through the water to their target some 500 yards away, they had barely armed themselves when they hit their target. Emerson had put Thomas on the scope so he could see the hit. Thomas cried out that the destroyer was broken in half by the torpedoes, and that the crew and survivors were jumping over the sides. He searched around to see a destroyer heading directly down their bow about two thousand yards away. He asked the Captain to let him fire on this one. Emerson quickly agreed and told the Diving Officer that he would need to get them down as soon as he heard the tubes being fired.

The XO called for Tubes Five and Six to be made ready. As soon as this was confirmed, he ordered final bearing and range. Finding the sleek greyhound was now only at 1000 yards and closing quickly, the XO called out, "Fire. All ahead full, right full rudder. Take her down to 200 feet."

The crew responded on command. They were getting better all the time now that they had some real practice. No one seemed overly concerned that the enemy was coming right down their throats, a maneuver that would have struck terror into their hearts a few days before.

They heard the results of their latest feat. The explosion was deafening as the destroyer was almost on top of where they were when they fired as it caught at least one of the torpedoes head on.

"Let's take a look," said Emerson with considerable calm. "You take the attack scope and I'll take the big one. Bring us up to 65 feet. Steady on course. Hold our speed."

What they saw amazed them. The destroyer had the front one-third of its hull blown away. The torpedo must have ignited an ammunitions hold. They were trying to get away from the area even as their forward motion seemed to be trying to make a submarine out of them, dragging them under. Skip and Curt agreed there was no sense in wasting another torpedo on that one. It would definitely not make it back to port. The lifeboats were already going over the side that they could see.

There was carnage all around. None of the escorts was left untouched. All were sunk or listing and on fire. The second freighter was about to slip under the surface. All that was left of the convoy was flotsam and bodies of crewmembers, both alive and dead.

Emerson decided to clear the area before surfacing. Just as they did so, they spotted a glint in the sky, some reflection off the sun on the horizon. They were still among the scattered mess and doubted that they would be seen, but determined that this was the aircraft the convoy had been promised, too little, too late.

CHAPTER SIXTEEN

They received orders that night from ComSubPac. Snook was to break off from Wolfpack One and proceed to the area between Okinawa and Kyushu Island, Japan. More specifically they were to spend the next fourteen days on "Operation Lifeguard" between Tanega Shima on the north and O Shima on the south. Their general position would be given to both the Air Force on Okinawa and any Navy aircraft carriers in the area, effective two days hence.

There was great joy aboard the U.S.S. Snook. They had successfully completed the patrol and were being extended to try out the radio equipment and floating whip antenna that had been installed at Pearl Harbor. Now they would get to see if it really worked as planned.

Captain Emerson called for a course change to 085 to head them east to their new patrol area. He asked the officers to meet him in the Wardroom in fifteen minutes.

"Gentlemen," he began, "We have been highly successful on this patrol. We have proven the merits of Wolfpack formations in driving the enemy shipping toward one another, and diverting attention from one evading submarine by the intrusion of another submarine. We have also learned some lessons about the difficulties of working in a Wolfpack where our independence is given up and our destiny is controlled by others. The information on these issues will be the subject of considerable discussion when we get back to Pearl. I ask that each of you record your thoughts and feelings while they are fresh in your mind. I would like to see a copy of what you have to say, so please have those records on my desk within 48 hours.

"Now we are heading closer to the Japanese coast to take up patrol between Okinawa and Kyushu. We will be testing our new radio equipment and the floating whip antenna. I am going to ask Mr. Thomas to brief you on this portion of our patrol since he acted as the project commander with SubPac on this concept, which was largely his answer to the problems of communications we have experienced in the past."

"Thanks, Captain. I think you all know about the installations we accomplished at Pearl and the meetings we had with the Admiral's staff and with the joint leadership of the Army Air Force and Navy carrier folks. We now have a dedicated receiver mounted in the Radio Shack and Hap Henry is keeping one ear tuned to it. We have an antenna system that we can deploy while still under the water, but close to the surface, that will send out a ribbon antenna trailing behind us on the surface. That antenna can be used during the daytime when we cannot surface.

"We can recover the antenna if we can surface, at which time it will be restored for future release. We can also cut the antenna free in case we believe that its detection topside would lead to our discovery. The materials and connection are not strong enough to allow us to drag it underwater, so if we have to go deep, we will disconnect it from the Radio Shack. We do have two extra antennas to install, and the installation takes about twenty minutes of surface time.

"So much for the technical side. From an operational standpoint, we are no longer pursuing the enemy shipping. We will do nothing that would jeopardize our location. 'Operation Lifeguard' is an essential element of the attacks on the Japanese mainland. As the number of aircraft sent over Japan are increased, we know the coastal fortifications will hit some of them. The Air Force and carriers operating out of this area know our assigned operating area and the emergency radio frequencies. We will get messages directly from aircraft pilots who must ditch their planes, or from flight controllers on aircraft carriers or land installations. Our job is to get to those aviators before the enemy, the weather, or the sharks.

"Prior attempts of submarines to provide pickup services have been dismal. Because they could not see us, the aviators were prone to head for surface ships, even though their aircraft were often unable to make it to those locations. The communications from the flight controllers through 'official' channels to Pearl Harbor and back to us were subject to time delays and misunderstandings of where the planes were ditched. By the time a submarine found the downed aviator, it was often too late, and we became a last resort body pick-up team.

"Now all that has changed. If we can prove that 'Operation Lifeguard' works, we will provide the salvation for these aviators. The enemy shipping will not know we are here, but the aviators will. Please let your department personnel know how essential this mission is, and thank them, in advance, for their participation." The XO lifted his coffee cup in a toast to this new adventure.

"Please inform your department personnel of their parts in this mission," said Emerson. "The Gunnery Department that has been so patient with us, and who have been wanting to get to the topside guns, will have their chance to do so. Once we get a signal about a plane being ditched, we will race to that location and surface. While we're on the surface, we will be vulnerable to air attack, and will need to have the guns manned fulltime. The gunners will be the first up and the last down while we are on the surface.

"We will try to use the forward deck for our operations. That way, the Bridge can keep control of the operations, while still navigating the boat. The rubber lifeboat will be inflated and kept under the deck next to the forward escape hatch. As we bring the aviators aboard, we will take them down that hatch into the Forward Torpedo Room where our 'Doc' will be standing by to give them any medical attention they need.

"Since we have used most of the torpedoes in the forward room, there should be room to house the aviators there. We will have to hang loose on that issue, depending upon how many we pick up, their medical condition, and their rank. We may have to use some of our berthing and may have to 'hot bunk' until we offload them. We expect to transfer any aviators we take on board onto an aircraft carrier within two days of pickup. If that is not possible, we will steam back to Okinawa. Either way, the aviators will not be with us long.

"Well, that about wraps it up. Any questions?" Hearing none, Skip assured the officers that there was much that they did not know, and that they would have further sessions like this to air out any problems or concerns.

Curt Thomas lingered behind as the fellow officers headed for their assigned departments to spread the word. "How do you think they took it? They have had a while to think about our mission out here, but I have not heard many questions."

"I think," responded Skip, "that they are reserving judgment. They want to see how it works before they commit themselves. I think they all want for it to work. They join us in hoping this will be the solution needed to save lives of fliers. They want to be a part of something special, something they can tell their children about someday. But they want to be a part of a winner."

"Don't we all? I guess I'm just a little nervous about this thing, because I was so involved that I may miss the forest and just see the trees. Too much attention to detail can dull your senses for the big picture. Fortunately, Skip, I know that you will keep us focused on that aspect of the mission."

It did take them the best part of two days to get on station, midway between the islands that formed the northern and southern extremities of their patrol area. Everyone used this time for catching up on the sleep lost the past week, and for repairing those pieces of equipment that could not be interrupted during the offensive maneuvers.

Hap Henry reported that the special receiver had been quiet, other than the radio checks received every four hours to make sure the equipment was working. He was anxious to deploy the floating antenna to see that it worked after the shocks they were subjected to, from the depth charges and explosions they had endured.

"This is your Captain speaking," Emerson said as he held the microphone to the 1MC general announcing system in his right hand, and looked at the notes he held in his left. "We have arrived in the patrol area to which we were assigned for 'Operation Lifeguard' and will commence that mission immediately. As a part of Wolfpack One we were working with two other submarines on an offensive maneuver intended to disrupt and sink enemy shipping, especially those ships carrying war materials to the Japanese islands. We were extremely successful in sinking merchant ships and their man-of-war escort destroyers. We proved that the Wolfpack concept could work. After one of us fired upon the enemy and was forced to take evasive actions, another submarine would take the attack and draw the escorts away. This has made our evasive procedures very effective. As something that the enemy has never seen before, we have the advantage of 'hide and seek' that future Wolfpacks may not have.

"But now we will not be an offensive unit. We will not search out enemy shipping. Our sole reason for this part of the mission is to save lives of aviators who must abandon their aircraft because they have been hit while making their bombing raids on the mainland. In order to be effective, we will be silent. We will surface at night to charge our batteries or move to a new area. We will stay submerged during the daylight hours unless we are picking up a survivor. If we are on the surface during daylight hours our gunners will constantly man the deck guns to defend us from air attacks. We must get to the downed airmen as soon as we can, to avoid their loss to enemy ships, sharks, or adverse sea conditions.

"I know that I can count on each of you to do your part in this important mission. Many of you are aware that we are trying some new radio and antenna concepts for the war Department. If they work for us, we will be the model for other submarines to follow. Like anything else that is new, there is much we do not know. We will be working together as a team to make things happen for the best. I have every confidence in your abilities. Thank you and Godspeed."

Captain Emerson set the microphone back into its cradle. He hoped the men were inspired by his message, in addition to the briefing the department officers would have concluded by this time. He was proud of his crew and his submarine. He knew they would support his direction. He wanted the crew to know of his pride in them.

In the Forward Torpedo Room, Second Class Petty Officer Clem Moore reflected the feelings of some of his colleagues. "Sheeeet. Here we go again. Guess anything is bedder than that 'gang bang' back there in China Sea. I jess know we're goin to fight over who gets credit for those sinkins. Bet I know who gets to clean up the mess after thos fly-boys is hauled down through our compartment. On any other Navy ship, I'd be rankin enlisted. On this pig boat I'm the junior guy with the shit details."

"Oh, knock it off, Moore," responded Chief Edwards. "I'm tired of yer cryin about everythin. If'n ya want a transfer, I can accommodate ya. We can get you signed to one of dose P.T. boats at some little island out here. Ya'll be surrounded by plywood and pounded so hard yer head will be restin on yer shoulders. Then ya'll really have sompen to bitch about."

"Yeah, well at least I'd have some seaman to clean up my mess. Somen to boss round like you boss me round. An des here dolphins might get som looks from dos cute island gals."

Chief Edwards thought about it. Clem Moore was all huff and no puff. When they got back to port, Clem would beg off of a transfer. He just liked to belly ache, but he did the job when the chips were down. There are probably several men on the sub who felt the same way, but wouldn't say anything. Those were the ones to worry about. He always knew how Moore felt about things.

The first day on station was uneventful. It was Sunday and the allied forces were resting up for a busy week ahead. The war in Europe was concluding. And the added troops in the Pacific were making a difference in the retreat of the Japanese forces off the islands they had occupied and back to their mainland. Now they were finding that even that stronghold was under attack. And fewer of their merchant ships were getting to the motherland with the needed war materials and with the supplies that kept their nation alive.

CHAPTER SEVENTEEN

The "Pretty Lady" bounced along at 8000 feet, the weather conditions causing the B-25 to shimmy her way to Japan. Bomber Squadron 135 had just moved onto Okinawa two weeks prior. This was their fourth mission to Japan with a load of incendiary bombs. There were seven men in this crew: pilot, copilot, bombardier, nose gunner, tail gunner, and two belly gunners. Major Steve Ellinswood was the pilot. He had been flying B-25s for two years. This crew was just assembled after they got reassigned to Okinawa, but the pilot and copilot had been together for a year, and had ferried the plane from Hickam Air Base where it had been shipped to after seeing action in the European front. Steve loved flying and thought the 25s were the best bombers in the air. He had started flying back in Colorado where his uncle kept a Stearman biplane on his ranch. He was eight years old when Uncle Ted had first turned the controls over to him and let him fly the plane. He was hooked from that day on, and looked forward to earning his wings after college. He managed to get in two years of college when the war broke out. He was offered a commission and sent to flight training school at Colorado Springs. Then he was assigned to Hickam Air Base for bomber training where he had been for the two years, running sorties on barren atolls and bombing the hell out of them.

Captain George Smith was the copilot. George like working with Steve Ellinswood. They had met at Hickam and had been flying together ever since. George was a newcomer to flying, but found it to be contagious. The more he flew, the more he looked forward to flying. Smith was a country boy from South Carolina, but he and Ellinswood were like two brothers in the way they thought about things. They had ferried the "Pretty Lady" from Oahu, stopping at Midway, Wake, and Guam to refuel before getting to Okinawa. Each pilot trusted the other with his life. That made flying easy, because one could sleep while the other flew. Both pilots were needed during an attack mission, but the plane was easy for one person to fly when they were just traveling between points.

Lieutenant Peter Johnson had wanted to be a pilot, but had been diverted to bombardier school because he failed the early in-plane tests. He was a crack bombardier that Ellinswood and Smith were proud to have on their team. He held the highest scores for direct hits of anyone else in the Squadron.

The enlisted airmen who rounded out the flight crew included Sergeant Jack Reilly who manned the nose gun; Sergeant Tom Dean as the tail gunner; and Corporals Ted Tower and Terry Black who were the left and right side belly gunners. These four men, under the direction of Sergeant Reilly who was the senior enlisted man in the crew, also made sure the plane was ready for flight and monitored the actions of the ground crew mechanics.

The "Pretty Lady" crew was assigned soon after arrival at Okinawa. They trained together for seven days before they undertook their first sortie. During the second week, they had successfully completed three flights over the southern mainland of Kyushu, one to the port city of Kagoshima and the other two up the coast to Nagasaki.

Their B-25 bomber was exactly the same as those flown by General Jimmie Doolittle only a few months earlier, when Doolittle flew off an aircraft carrier and surprised the Japanese with the first United States aerial attack on the mainland. Because they could not land on the aircraft carrier and the allied forces had not yet taken nearby islands, the planes in Doolittle's "Shangri La" Squadron had to try to get to China or were forced to ditch their aircraft at sea. Now the bombing attacks were island based and the number of missions increased every day.

They had been airborne for 90 minutes getting to their target. Once they flew over the coast, the flak from gun emplacements started. The closer they came to the seaport, the heavier the flak. Their mission on this day was the shipyard, with ships as primary targets and warehouses as secondary targets. They had dropped down to 5000 feet to make sure that Pete Johnson could get a clear view through his sights. During the bombing run, the bombardier was, in fact, in charge of the flight. The pilots did what he ordered. The aircraft became a bombing platform until "bombs away" at which time the pilots took control and made whatever evasive maneuvers they could.

"We are coming onto target," said Pete Johnson. "Hold her steady on speed and course. Open the bomb bay doors."

"The doors are open and locked," responded Captain Smith. "We have visual confirmation from the gunners. We are steady as the flak will let us be. Go get 'em Pete."

"Bombs away." The eight incendiary bombs dropped out of the bay in pairs and headed for the targets.

"Let's get out of here, George," hollered Steve Ellinswood. He crammed the throttles on the four Lycoming engines to the stops and hit the rudder with his left foot as he turned the steering yoke to the left. The big plane banked left as it picked up speed. The pilot pushed the yoke and their nose went down enough to help them build up the speed they needed.

Below them, the flashes of the bombs hitting grabbed their attention. Two ships were the recipients of four bombs, and the rest were scattered across the wharf to the closest building that was engulfed in flames. These bombs did not have the explosive charges of some bombs, but were filled with jelly-like petroleum distillates that added to their ignition power and caused the flames to be dispersed.

Just as they were completing their turn to head back toward the coast, they were hit in the left side. Both engines on that wing caught fire and Ted Tower reported that Terry Black had been hit. Major Ellinswood and Captain Smith were both working to maintain control of their plane.

As they feathered the props on the left engines and gave more boost to the starboard engines, Ellinswood hollered, "Hey, Pete, take a look at Black to see how bad it is. Smith and I are going to assess our damages and see if we can get back to base. We're clear of the coastline now so we should not have additional flak. Let's hope the Zero's don't show up for a while.

"What is your fix, George?" he called to the copilot.

"I hit the fire extinguishers and doused the fire, but I don't think we can use those engines again. There is considerable oil leaking from each of them. We seem to be holding our reduced speed with the two engines on the right side. The temperature gauges are going up, so I don't know how long they can take the load."

"Let's throttle back to just enough speed to keep us up here. The Squadron controllers know of our dilemma and are asking whether we can make it. They have reminded me that we have ditch instructions if we can't get back there."

Pete Johnson appeared from the rear of the airplane, his face ashen. "He's dead. Poor guy never had a chance. The shell hit the engine closest to him and parts of it slicked him up pretty badly. Tower is going to be all right now. He was a little hysterical until we got Black's body out of his chair and covered up.

"The oil is streaking back from each of the engines all along the left wing. We are lucky they did not shoot the wing off. These big mothers don't fly well with only one wing, I am told. What are we going to do, Skipper?"

"Somewhere out there is a submarine that is supposed to pick us up if we have to ditch. We don't see anything on the surface, so hopefully they are listening for our call. I think we had better get as far back toward Okinawa as we can before we ditch. Were you able to see if the life boat is O.K.?"

"It is torn to shreds. I looked at it while I was back there. Looks to me like we get to swim."

"Even more reason to get as far away from Japan as possible before we go down. Who knows where that submarine is and how long it will take them to get to us." Major Ellinswood picked up the transmitter and asked Captain Smith to dial up the emergency frequency. "Mayday, Mayday. This is "Pretty Lady" coming down for a swim. We have seven including one dead. We are heading for 28 X 25, Code Alpha, and will ditch at 0931 local."

A surface ship would have answered him, but the orders for the submarines called for silence. The aviators could only hope they were being heard. They were committed now to a time and place they were going to splash their B-25. Ellinswood was going to take advantage of the fairly calm waters to do a belly flop stall that, he hoped, would give them time on the surface to get everybody, including their dead colleague, off before she went down to Davey Jones' locker.

They managed to further reduce their speed and were at 150 knots and 1000 feet when they approached their designated spot. Time had run out and it was now or never. "Together, George, we will cut the engines and, when I say so, you pull back on your yoke with me. We are going to try to stall just above the waves to give us as little headway when we hit the water as we can.

"Everybody buckle up and stand by. As soon as we hit the water, get out away from the plane and inflate your jackets." The crew, other than the two pilots, was assembled in the mid section of the plane, ready to jump. Lt. Johnson and Sergeant Dean would jump together with Black's body between them.

The maneuver worked. They were almost at a dead stop when they belly flopped into the water. The plane floated long enough for the men to get into the water and away from the fuselage. These big bombers were not made to float for long, and the water was gushing into the cavity within seconds. With one big 'burp,' the plane went under. Major Ellinswood called out and each crewmember responded. They were all accounted for, even the body of their lost crewmember.

They had not been alone in the water more than fifteen minutes when they heard a noise, a giant hissing sound. An enormous gray hull started to emerge near them, and they were startled until they realized it was their rescue submarine surfacing.

The U.S.S. Snook had been on station for its second night. It was moving slowly along on the surface with its regular whip antenna extended and listening to the distress frequencies. All was quiet out there. Near dawn, the Bridge lookouts heard and then saw a squadron of bombers heading north toward Japan. If there was going to be a problem, it would come later that morning.

They dove as the sun came over the horizon to a brilliant cloudless day. After setting their compensating balances in the trim tanks, the Captain ordered them to periscope depth. At 65 feet, they could deploy the floating whip antenna and still know if they needed to take a look, they could stick their periscope up without changing depths. There was a slight chop to the sea surface that would keep them from being detected this close to the surface, unless some slow moving aircraft were to be looking for them.

It was shortly after 0900 that the Radio Shack came alive with the "Mayday" message. Hap Henry called for the Captain or XO to validate the coded ditching area part of the message. They were so close to that area they would have to watch out that they didn't skewer the airplane on their periscope.

As the clock ticked off the minutes, the Captain stationed himself on the larger scope and the XO stayed in the Radio Shack relaying any further instructions to the Conning Tower. At 0925, the Captain reported that he could see the aircraft moving very slowly toward their position. The left wing down configuration assured him that it was "Pretty Lady" he was seeing, not some Japanese Betty out trying to disrupt the rescue operation.

He watched the evacuation of the aviators, and waited until the aircraft slid beneath the surface before turning the submarine toward the awaiting men. As they surfaced, the gun crew was ordered topside along with the rescue team. Double lookouts went into the periscope shears to keep an alert watch for aircraft.

The floating antenna had worked! It was draped across the after deck now as the sub maneuvered toward the men in the sea. The Captain hoped the propellers could not snag the antenna, but it seemed to end just short of the housing for the screws. Skip Emerson was reminded of the arguments pro and con on the length of the antenna. The Air Force was insistent that it be long enough for a full wavelength; Hap Henry was sure they could do just as well with a half wavelength. The Captain was now sure that if the Air Force had gotten its way, their antenna would be gone right now, and maybe wrapped around the props causing some other problems.

The rescue crew had the six live and one dead aviators aboard and down the forward hatch within twelve minutes. He ordered the gunnery detail below, and then called the lookouts down from the shears. They submerged quietly and without incident. That was O.K. with Emerson.

After they were settled back into their periscope depth, he asked the XO to take the Conn and he headed forward to meet their first rescued men. He introduced himself to the Major and his men. "Welcome aboard. I'm Lieutenant Commander Charles Emerson, the Captain of the U.S.S. Snook. We are pleased to be your hosts until we get you back to Okinawa or to a transfer ship. We are happy to find that you are not too water logged. It was indeed fortunate that you splashed down where you did, because it minimized our exposure on the surface. We join in your sorrow for your fallen colleague. If there is anything we can do to make you comfortable, please let me know."

"Our heartfelt thanks to you and your crew, Captain," responded Major Ellinswood, "We were fearful when we could not see you as we were preparing to ditch. We were more fearful when you surfaced so near to us. We weren't sure what kind of monster made the noises that came out of your ship as you came up. The six of us will be a testimony to the use of submarines in these rescue operations."

The medic had brought a body bag for the dead man and they were preparing to move the bag to the freezer. The men were given dry clothing while theirs were put into the dryer that had been installed in the Forward Torpedo Room just for this purpose. The visitors were told they must stay in the Forward Torpedo Room unless they were escorted by one of the ship's personnel. They would be heading back toward Okinawa as soon as the other planes in the Squadron were safely on their way back to their home base. There was no surface ship in the area to which they could be transferred, so Snook would leave the area long enough to get these aviators back to their base.

The Snook stayed on station most of the day and set course for Okinawa at 1600, moving at four knots submerged until sunset, at which time they surfaced and made turns for 21 knots. They were less than 100 miles from the coastal port on Okinawa so Captain Emerson planned to get there, offload the aviators, and be back at sea before dawn. The Air Force personnel tried to talk the crew into staying at Okinawa for the day. Tempting as it was, the Snook had been assigned to lifeguard duty at a swimming pool that was open day and night. It would not do for them to be in Okinawa when they were needed out at sea. Skip Emerson had to admit to himself that he would like to have spent at least one evening on the beach.

They dropped their rescued airmen on the pier and made arrangements for the body to be transferred to the base morgue. Then they were underway, anxious to clear the breakwater and get to deep water before sunrise. It took most of the day, running submerged, to get back to the station area where they were expected to be in case another plane had to ditch.

The next three days were uneventful. Most of the missions were coming from aircraft carriers stationed further to the east of their location. The few flights out of Okinawa were, fortunately, successful in their return to their base.

In addition, the Navy had brought in some PBYs. These "flying boats" could get to the downed aviators quickly, land near them for pickup, and get them back to their station quickly. These aircraft were a threat to the submarine mission, but they could not operate where there were any enemy ships or aircraft. They were under armed, sitting ducks on the water, and flew too slowly to get away from any attack planes in the air. They were great for mid ocean rescues away from war zones. The Navy strategy was evolving into one that used the PBY and surface ships away from the heat of battle, and relied on submarines to do the pickups where the others could not, in the midst of the fighting. No one seemed to be too concerned for the jeopardy created for the submarines that still had to surface and expose themselves during the rescue.

Over the course of the next four days, they recovered three fighter pilots and a duo from a fighter-bomber. These five aviators were transferred to a frigate for return to the U.S.S. Forrestal from which they had flown their planes.

At the end of the patrol time, the score for the U.S.S. Snook was twelve rescues, a pretty good record for trying something new, they all had to agree. The crew was jubilant when the Captain announced late one afternoon on their fourteenth day on station that they were going to head home that evening. They knew they had done a great job and the test of the new radio and antenna was successful. Even Torpedoman Clem Moore, who had complained about the mess he was going to inherit, had to admit he had enjoyed meeting the airmen and getting to know what their part in the war was all about.

CHAPTER EIGHTEEN

The U.S.S. Snook arrived at Pearl Harbor to find both U.S.S. Sargo and U.S.S. Stingray already in port. The three boats were tied up at adjoining piers, and members of the Stingray, with whom they shared opposite sides of a pier, were there to handle their lines and help secure them to the pier. Captain Steve Gallagher, the Wolfpack One Commander, was there at the head of the pier to greet Snook. He was accompanied by Captain Phillip Brannigan and Commander Fred Fleming from ComSubPac who were anxious to talk about 'Operation Lifeguard.'

Skip Emerson had hoped to get ComSubPac to talk about the Wolfpack concept before Gallagher got to them, but realized that would not be possible. He waved to the men at the head of the pier, but his eyes were searching the small crowd of well-wishers to see if he could spot Nance. He had no idea whether anyone would call to let her know he was arriving. Then he spotted her, standing in the shade of a palm tree off to the side of the crowd. She caught his eyes and that radiant smile captivated him. He almost forgot what they were doing for a minute.

Skip Emerson stepped over the side of the Bridge, and used the footholds to climb down onto the deck. Saluting the flag, he stepped up onto the gangplank and crossed to the pier heading to where Nance was standing. He quickly paid his respects to the SubPac people and set a time for a debriefing tomorrow morning. Then he turned his full attention to the lady that filled his dreams.

Their long embrace felt heavenly to Skip. He was oblivious to the surroundings. It was only when Nance whispered in his ear that he realized there were others who wanted to share his attention. Together, Nance and Skip walked into the crowd that awaited the crew. He spoke to as many people as he recognized, and some that he didn't. He thanked them for showing their support and told them he was proud of the crew and all that had been accomplished. Crewmembers introduced him to wives and sweethearts that were there to greet their return.

Curt Thomas came up the pier and stopped to talk with them. Skip told Curt of the debriefing meeting set for the next day, and suggested that they have breakfast together to map out what they wanted to get across in the initial meeting. Curt said he was going to hang around the boat for a while, and suggested that Skip and Nance might want to get away early. Knowing there was nothing that could not wait until the next day, Skip agreed and joined Nance as they walked up to where he had left the assigned jeep.

"Your place or mine?" asked Skip as they climbed into the vehicle.

"Let's go down to the beach. Your apartment there is all ready for you. I took the liberty of letting the hotel management know you were arriving this morning so they have it all ready for you. It is so handy to the beach and all the places we love to go."

They stopped at the liquor store near the base entrance to pick up some rum and mixes. Then they threaded their way through the noonday traffic on Kam highway heading into Honolulu and on to Waikiki. They turned off Kaulakaua Boulevard and into the parking lot beside the Royal Hawaiian. Skip could feel the tingling anticipation of his body at the thought of what would come next.

Skip quickly checked in, grabbed the key and raced out to the car to get Nance. Each of them tried to act casually, even though their hearts were racing. Skip locked the door behind them and they fell into each other's arms. A long embrace turned into a torrent of passion. They fell across the bed and hurriedly undressed one another, trying to maintain their embrace while doing so. The hunger for love was insatiable as they clung to one another and caressed each other. Skip found the taut nipples with his fingertips and guided his mouth to their sweetness. Nance fondled Skip into a hardness she had only remembered in her dreams. As she drew him inside her, she shuddered at the exquisite feel.

"Oh, Skip, let's never leave this room. I miss you so much and yearn for your return when you are away."

"I know because I feel the same way about you, Nance. This is what keeps me going out there at sea. Knowing that I have you to come back to makes it all worth it. One day we will know that we don't have to be apart anymore. Until that time, let us cherish what time we have together."

"Let's do it again, then. Can you?"

"I've been saving up for this. Just watch me." He started at her forehead and ran his tongue lightly around her eyes, down the center of her nose to her mouth that he entered with a fury. Then he ventured down her neck lingering at her breasts, before trailing down to her navel. By this time, Nance was moaning and asking for more. They made love more passionately that they had the first time.

Now it was her turn. She started with his toes and worked her way up his calves to his knees. Then she explored the inner parts of his thighs. "How does that feel, big boy?" she teased. Once again they made mad, passionate love to one another. Afterward they slept as neither had slept since they were last together.

Skip stirred from his sleep and looked at the watch he had put on the bedside table. He realized they had been asleep for almost four hours. He kissed Nance's eyes and said, "Hello. Is anyone in there?"

He started the shower and she joined him. The steaming hot water felt so good. Skip was reminded that the submarine regulation "wet down, wash down, rinse down" shower could never take the place of this soaking enjoyment. It didn't hurt that he had such a pleasurable companion in the shower with him.

"Where shall we go for dinner?" he asked. "Do you have any ideas?"

"I heard about a great café in Kaneohe. Do you feel like driving around to the windward side of the island?"

"Sure. It's another beautiful afternoon. The ride will feel good. They dressed in shorts and aloha shirts. With their native thongs on their feet, they could almost pass for locals. They stuffed their swim suits and towels into a bag, just in case they decided that some cove was just too inviting, and off they went.

They headed south past Diamond Head remembering the great time they had at Hanauma Bay, and slowed to observe the Blow Hole spout its well-wishes to them. They continued around the southern point of Oahu and followed the curving road back toward the northern windward side of the island. Kaneohe Bay was a beautiful, if remote, part of the island. It had been a village inhabited by locals only until the Marines decided to build an Air Base there. Now it was a bustling community where fifty percent of the population was in uniform.

Kaneohe Bay was a large shallow bowl open to the ocean beyond its coral reef that provided the protection for its fishing boats. The locals gathered longusta, the Hawaiian lobster, in this bay. Longusta was a delicacy the Kaneohe Café offered as its specialty. Skip and Nance ordered the house salad and broiled longusta.

"How was your trip? Did you accomplish what you set out to do?"

"Very successful, Nance. We were part of the first efforts to operate in a Wolfpack of three submarines for the first two weeks, and then we broke off to operate by ourselves to test the radio communications system for the last two weeks. We picked up three solo flyers and seven members of a bomber crew. And the radio system was almost flawless. We are having a big meeting at SubPac headquarters tomorrow morning and I expect the outcome will be to put our equipment on several other submarines and expand 'Operation Lifeguard' further up around the Japanese coastline."

"Isn't that awfully dangerous? The Japanese must be fearful to have you so close to their mainland. Won't they send out ships to try to sink you?"

"Sure they will, but it is essential that we save the lives of those flyers. Surface ships can't get as close to the mainland as we can. We are careful not to be detected, although most of our pickups have been in the daylight. For a while, we are still unknown and that helps. Once the enemy knows we are out there, it will be a different story."

"That is spooky to me. I'll be so glad when it is all over and you come back for good. They told us at the hospital yesterday, that any military officers who are foreign nationals can apply for United States citizenship that will be automatically conferred because of our military service. I am going to do that so I will be a U.S. citizen soon. I've decided that I would never be happy to live back in Guam again. Now that I've seen Hawaii and met you, I know this is the life for me."

"Let's toast to your becoming an American citizen," Skip said holding his glass of beer up. They toasted and downed their beers. Skip ordered another round. Their dinners came and they launched into eating them, both hungry from their earlier activities.

They left the café two hours later, full and contented. They had decided to drive up the windward side a ways. The late afternoon sun was interrupted by a blustery cloud formation that dropped some rain on them. "That is why it is more tropical on this side, where lush plants need more water," Skip said, always amazed that two minutes after it rained, the bright sunshine was back and the steam was rising off the pavement on the roadway. Skip drove carefully along the ribbon highway that was used more for foot travel than for vehicles. The locals sometimes herded their sheep from one location to another along this highway. A driver needed to stay on his toes.

As they rode along, Nance talked about her job and how busy they were getting, as the outlying medical facilities were being centralized at Tripler Hospital. As the roads were constructed joining the outlying parts of Oahu, it was no longer necessary for each military base to maintain its own hospital. The Navy at Pearl Harbor and Barbers Point; the Army at Schofield Barracks; the Army Air Force at Hickam; and the Marines at Kaneohe—all of these could get to Tripler in a fairly short drive, except for Kaneohe that could only be accessed by going around the southern tip of the island, or over the Pali. The Pali Road was a slow and rigorous journey over the mountain ridge that separated the leeward side from the windward side of Oahu. It would not be appropriate for someone needing medical attention. A small hospital contingent was located at the Kaneohe Marine Base for trauma patients, but any long-term attention would still be diverted to Tripler.

Skip interrupted Nance to point out a cove with a quiet sandy beach. He suggested they stop and get wet. He parked the jeep in the sand alongside the road and they headed through the tropical rushes onto the beach area. The high tide hid any debris that might have been left on the beach, and it looked as though they were the first humans to have ever ventured here. The sand was unblemished in its slope down into the water. The ocean was an emerald green as far out as the group of tiny islands that poked up out of the sea, breaking some ten kilometers off the beach.

Nance grabbed her swimsuit and wandered off toward the nearby rushes to change. Skip thought, what the hell. He stripped off his shorts and shirt right there and put on his swim trunks. He folded his clothes and put them atop the bag from which they had taken their swimsuits and towels. Nance came walking out of the rushes with that strut of a model walking down the runway, and dropped her clothes on top of his. Then, before he could speak, she raced for the water, screaming, "Come on, sailor, let's get wet."

Skip obliged and ran after her. She flitted across the light surf and plunged into a rolling wave. The wave dissolved itself and there she was lying on the sand in water too shallow to take her anywhere. Skip held out a hand and laughed. He was reminded of their first meeting when he had done almost the same thing. Fortunately, she was not hurt. There had been enough water in the wave to cushion her from the sand impact. They both laughed and, hand in hand, waded into the deeper water.

The bottom was smooth and soft to the touch of their feet. The water temperature matched the air temperature at 76 degrees. Swimming in this tepid water was like being suspended in space. Skip dove down to the bottom to see what he could find for Nance and came up with a large Conch shell. It was the kind the natives used as horns to announce their communal gatherings. Skip rinsed and drained it and took it up on the beach where their clothes bag was. He rejoined Nance in the water and they swam together out to a corral reef and back into the shore.

Nance spread out their towels and they lay down to soak up some of the late afternoon sun before it settled behind the mountain ridge that divided Oahu like a protruding spine of an ancient dinosaur.

CHAPTER NINETEEN

S kip and Nance awoke early the next day. Nance had the early shift at Tripler and needed to be at her unit by 0715. Skip had promised Phil Brannigan that he would meet with him before the scheduled meeting on the success of 'Operation Lifeguard' for a discussion on the Wolfpack concept.

The starched khakis were stiff as a board and Skip found himself bending and turning to loosen them up while he waited for Nance to finish dressing. Skip had ordered coffee from room service, and they each had decided to wait for breakfast at their respective appointments. As they headed for Tripler, Nance talked about the new staff that were coming into her department with the consolidation plan. They were also getting additional caseloads from the other hospitals, so the added staff did not mean any relief to the workload. Nance liked what she was doing and was proud of her profession. She had always dreamed of being a nurse and this was a dream fulfilled with the opportunity to come to Hawaii for training and assignment as an added bonus.

Skip talked about the meeting they would be having late in the morning. He was still wrestling with the issue of the Wolfpacks. "I don't want to alienate SubPac from this Washington idea, but I have to let them know that none of their submarine commanders like being subservient to anyone when we are out there. There is too much risk involved. And yet, I'd be the first to agree that we were successful in pulling the enemy off one another by our surprise torpedo firings. The enemy was clearly confused thinking there was only one submarine out there. Just when they were sure they had pinned us down, torpedoes coming from another submarine led them to believe that we were somewhere else."

"You just have to be honest with yourself, Skip. Give them both sides of the story and see where it heads. I'm sure there are pros and cons in every issue. Someone has to weigh those pros and cons and make a determination as to what to do."

"The surprise element won't last long. The enemy will figure they were dealing with more than one submarine and we will lose that advantage soon. All in all, I'd rather b completely independent on my next patrol."

Skip dropped Nance at the hospital entrance and headed out for Pearl Harbor. He headed for the finger piers and the U.S.S. Snook to see how repairs were coming along and to share a bite of breakfast with the XO. He parked the jeep at the head of his pier, in the place designated for in-port Captains' vehicles. The piers and surrounding shops were a beehive of activity as the base personnel and ships' companies hurried to complete the necessary repairs so the boats could get back out on their next patrols. The Snook was no exception. Skip could see Hap Henry and several base personnel in the periscope shears checking on the antenna system. As he crossed the gangplank on the brow of the boat and turned toward the fantail where the ensign was deployed, Skip could see Lt. Farrell, the Engineering Officer, talking with his enginemen above the hatch leading down to the After Engine Room. COB Jones was directing two seamen who were fastened in boatswain chairs over the port bow, scraping away some deposits and making ready to paint that section.

After speaking briefly to the Petty Officer standing guard on the deck, Skip headed up onto the Bridge from which he could drop down into the Conning Tower and Control Room on the way to his quarters. In the Conning Tower, he observed the Quartermasters updating the ship's charts to reflect data on shifting sandbars in their operating areas. As he passed into the Control Room, he found the Interior Communications Electricians cleaning the umbilical of the gyrocompass, and doing the routine maintenance on the motor repeater system that was used to signal orders for speed and direction to and from the Maneuvering Room and the Control Room or Conning Tower from which the orders came.

In his stateroom he checked the daily logs and standing orders. All were in order indicating there had not been any anomalies since he left. The XO had left a message that he had an emergency he was taking care of and he would see Skip at SubPac later in the morning.

After a quick walkthrough of the boat, he climbed up the ladder in the After Torpedo Room and walked forward on the deck to the gangway, telling the watch that he was leaving, and saluting as he strode across to the pier.

At 0855 Skip was at ComSubPac headquarters talking with Yeoman Smith as Captain Brannigan invited him into his office. "Welcome, once again, Skip. The word is that you had a very successful patrol, both in the Wolfpack One and in the Operation Lifeguard missions."

"We were probably a lot more successful than the records will ever show."

"How's that?" Captain Brannigan was clearly puzzled by Skip's response.

"One of the problems with the Wolfpack is that we were each shooting at the same targets. I'm positive that three torpedoes were fired for each one that would have been fired had we been patrolling alone. Each independent submarine wanted to make sure of the sinking. Now, we are arguing over who gets to count the sinking as their own. Even when there was any agreement on who would fire first, the other two Captains did not want to risk losing the target.

"Another problem is that we do not like working as a team. All of our training, and our selection as submarine commanders, has been based on our independence of thought and action. We do not want someone second-guessing our decisions. We will not jeopardize our crews and our boats by having someone else making our decisions for us. With all due respect for Commander Gallagher, it will not work regardless of whom that person is. We all know of Steve Gallagher's reputation. He doesn't need to prove himself to us. He is a legend for his patrols early in the war. But these are different times. We are patrolling under different circumstances now. We, as a group of submarine commanders, are taking far greater risks with our boats than any of the earlier patrols. So why would you think that an older sub commander could make a better decision? Really, Phil, this is not about Steve Gallagher. We will feel the same about any person who is put in the position of commodore of a Wolfpack."

"Was there anything you think went well with the Wolfpack?" Phil Brannigan questioned, wanting to get a full account of the issue.

"Yes, the enemy had never faced multiple submarines before. When one of us would fire, he would come at us intending to pin us down and sink us. Then when another boat fired, the enemy became confused thinking the sub had evaded him and was firing from another location. The enemy destroyer would immediately stop depth charging our area and move after the last bearing. This made our evasive procedures very simple and allowed us to return to firing position quickly. We had greater success in sinking or damaging enemy war ships as a result of this operation, but it will not take long for the Japanese to catch on to the fact that there is more than one submarine out there. And once that fact is established, we will have lost our advantage. I'm saying, Captain Brannigan, that the advantage of the Wolfpack will not continue to be an advantage for very long. Once you take away this surprise, you are left only with the disadvantages of lack of independence and expending too many torpedoes. God knows, we have to be careful about how many torpedoes we use on any one target now, let alone using three times as many."

"Well, Skip, I'll tell you that several of your colleagues have told us similar concerns. I don't know what we will do, but we do appreciate the frankness with which you have provided us the necessary feedback we could never get from here. All we see is an increase in tonnage sunk. And, of course, we get glowing reports from the Commodores who are happy to be back in the thick of things."

"Just let me add," said Skip, "that the submarine skipper none of us want to be is the one on whose sub the Commodore is riding. Now there are two captains of that boat. I know that it isn't supposed to work that way, but it does. Every decision that captain makes is second-guessed by the Wolfpack leader. Every move, every call, is subject to another perspective. None of us deserve that. We have each done our time under someone else's command. Now it is our turn. Give us our orders and turn us loose."

Curt Thomas and Fred Fleming were talking with the team that worked on the floating whip antenna as Phil Brannigan and Skip Emerson joined them. Curt was briefing the others on the deployment and use of the antenna on the mission just completed. The floating whip had been successful and had stayed operational through several surfacing periods. Hap Henry had difficulty in replacing the antenna once it was damaged beyond use. One of the engineers said they had come up with another method to simplify the replacement of the antenna. The connectors were now molded so that the shipboard personnel did not have to resort to makeshift watertight connections.

On behalf of Admiral Pennington," Captain Brannigan intruded, "and all of us here at SubPac, I want to congratulate Commander Emerson, Lt. Thomas, Radioman Henry and the entire crew of the U.S.S. Snook for the outstanding leadership they have provided on 'Operation Lifeguard.' We now know it works and works well. We have been given permission to outfit four additional boats with the same kind of communications receivers and antennas. I am confident that many lives will be saved because of your diligence in looking at the problem and finding a solution."

Skip responded, "We also want to thank the SubPac engineering staff and base shipyard personnel who took our idea and made it work. We knew what to do. You knew how to do it. Together we have proven what positive teamwork can accomplish. Snook stands ready to go back out to try the fixes we have made in the past few days. And we will be happy to demonstrate our system to any other boats that are part of your designated retrofits."

As the meeting broke up, the men gave their personal thanks to those they had been working with. Curt Thomas and Fred Fleming spoke with the other engineers about some additional safeguards on the system.

Skip talked with Phil Brannigan about when their next orders might be issued. "The Admiral," said the Chief of Staff, "is leaning towards sending you back out on another 'Operation Lifeguard' mission. He wants more evidence that the floating whip can make a difference. I had been thinking about a Wolfpack in which each submarine would be equipped for lifeguard duty, but you have given me pause to rethink my position on the entire Wolfpack idea. Perhaps if we send you back out while we are retrofitting the three other subs with your communications gear and antenna system, you can give us the additional confirmation we need. And you would be out there by yourself, as you indicate is your preference.

"On another topic, Skip, even though I said I would not bring it back up, the rumor mill tells me you have a new love in your life. I saw the young medical officer awaiting your submarines arrival yesterday. Very pretty, I might add. And several of your colleagues have offered that they see a settling down in your personality. I should not, but I will tell you, that pleases many of us."

"Thanks, Phil. Nurse Nancy is the love of my life. She had been directly influencing my behavior after witnessing a near skirmish shortly after we met. It is clear to me that my behavior has to change if I am to find the soul mate I desire.

"And regarding the next mission, we would like that. My crew would rather be sinking enemy ships, but they are also dedicated to saving lives of aviators. They showed their abilities to do so on our last patrol. We stand ready to give you more positive evidence of how a submarine can play a vital role in sea rescues if that is what the Admiral wants."

"How soon could you be ready to go out on patrol?"

"We need another three days to complete our repairs and another day to load provisions. We could be underway in four days without pushing the men beyond their already tough schedules."

"Expect your orders tomorrow, calling for you to leave port on Monday morning. Once again, Skip, thank you for your frank observations." Phil Brannigan shook Skip's hand before they parted.

Skip spent the remainder of Thursday on board the Snook, attending to paper work and reports prepared by the ship's officers. He also signed some personnel requests for promotions and submarine qualifications. During the past patrol, four enlisted men became qualified as submariners, which allowed them to wear the coveted dolphins and use the 'SS' designation after their rank.

Five other crewmembers had taken fleet exams for promotion in enlisted rank and had passed their exams. This paperwork, when approved by SubPac would raise their pay and give them additional stripes on their uniforms. Two Petty Officer Second Class Electricians would become First Class; two Torpedoman Third Class would become Torpedoman Second Class; and one seaman would become Engineman Third Class. These promotions were the result of a lot of studying these men had accomplished during their off hours in the months before the examinations were held. Their department heads had attested to their personal qualifications for promotion, and the examinations attested to their knowledge. Skip asked Lt. J.G. Farley Worth, who was the Personnel Officer in addition to Commissary Officer, to take the papers up to ComSubPac that day so the men might get their promotions before the next patrol.

On Friday morning, Skip met with the ship's officers over breakfast in the Wardroom. He congratulated them on the success of the last patrol and the credited tonnage of enemy ships sunk by the Wolfpack One operation. He told them there were disputes by the sub commanders as to which sub sunk which ships, something they had talked about before, but that SubPac would make the final determinations based on the log books each submarine submitted, as to the times of each torpedo firing. Curt Thomas told his fellow officers about the 'fix' on the floating whip antenna and about the meeting he and the Captain had with the SubPac engineers.

"We are going back out on Monday," Skip announced, "to provide further evidence of our ability to save the lives of aviators. We will probably go alone, not as part of a Wolfpack. I have told SubPac of our concerns about the Wolfpacks as well as the good side. I believe there will be considerable discussion about the future of this approach. It may be that they will be used for a while to take advantage of the fact the enemy still has not figured out we were more than one submarine. We agree, however, that once the advantage of surprise is taken away, the lack of independence far outweighs any other advantages.

"I want each of you to get as much done today as possible. Stores will be delivered this afternoon. I am told the torpedoes are loaded aboard already. As soon as things are in place let every one else go for the weekend. And that means yourselves, as well. I want a fresh and dedicated crew ready to set sail Monday morning."

Each officer around the table gave his colleagues a quick briefing of his department. They were all excited about getting back out to sea. They were born warriors, proud of what they were doing. Skip was pleased, knowing the officers' excitement was contagious. The men in the departments would reflect their officer's feeling toward this next patrol.

Curt Thomas confirmed with Skip that he was going to be on board for the day and promised to leave a message at the Royal Hawaiian's front desk for Skip at the end of the day, letting him know that everything was set to go. Skip placed a call to Nance at the hospital to see if she could get off early, for a long weekend together.

Suspecting what this meant, Nance answered that she would find someone to cover for her. It was never a problem for the nurses who routinely covered for one another. She knew there would be plenty of time to pay back the person who covered her shift, while Skip was at sea. She could tell from his tone of voice that this was going to be the long weekend before he would be gone on another patrol. A nervous spasm chilled her spine. She thought about how it would be when the war was over and Skip never had to go out on these extended and dangerous missions anymore.

At 1230 Nance was standing outside the entrance to Tripler as she saw Skip driving up the long entranceway. The Hibiscus was in full bloom and their scent added to her jubilant mood. She was going to see to it that this was a memorable weekend for both of them.

As she hopped into the jeep, Skip leaned over and embraced her. "This is it," she said softly, "isn't it? You are going back out, aren't you?"

Skip was surprised. "How did you know that?"

"I could tell from your voice when you called. I don't know what it was, and it was not something you said. I think I have known you would be going back on patrol soon, so I was expecting this."

"Well, as usual, you're right. We leave Monday, but it looks like I am free until then. As long as no emergencies come up that Curt can't handle, and I can't imagine any, you and I have the weekend to ourselves."

And it was a glorious weekend. They frolicked in the sun. They made love, passionately. They went to their favorite restaurants. The drove around the island, stopping along the way for a swim at their favorite beach. They sat for hours on the beach on the North Shore, watching the giant breakers crash onto the sand. With the exception of a couple of quiet periods when each of them knew what the other was thinking, their moods were upbeat and happy. They enjoyed one another and knew they were lucky to be together.

"Nance," Skip said over dinner at the Willows restaurant on Saturday evening, "What would you say if I asked you to marry me? I know we had agreed to wait until the war is over, but I don't want to wait anymore. How about getting married when I get back from this patrol?"

"My heart says yes, Skip. I live for these times with you. When you are gone, I just drive myself at work to fill the time. When you are available, I just want to be with you. It doesn't matter what we do, just being together is what counts. I think we are about as ready as we are going to get."

"Maybe it will make the time go by more quickly, making all the arrangements for our wedding while I am gone."

"Yes it will. Oh! I'm excited now. My mind is flooding with a thousand different thoughts. Skip, you make me a very happy woman. I am so lucky to have found you there on that beach."

"It is I who feels fortunate to have been there at the right time. Someone would have come along for you, I am sure. I am just glad it was me. Those scratches and bruises were well worth it. You have given purpose to my life. You have, in the fairly short time we have been together, made me change and mature. I now have responsibility for my life, not just my actions as a Navy officer. It has been a wonderful transformation, and I owe it to you."

"You have changed. I have seen that. You were so full of anger when we first met. You had a short fuse and seemed ready to fight at any provocation. But that is gone now. You are full of love and praise for others. I see that in you, and it makes me even more proud to be a part of you life."

The rest of Saturday evening and all of Sunday were consumed with talk about their future life together. Skip wanted to stay in the Navy after the war. It was all he knew, and his engineering training at the Academy was not as interesting to him as was the management of people and the command of situations. Nance was interested in her nursing profession but would set it aside for being a mother when that time came.

Sunday evening's mood was pensive but the overriding feeling was love. They were going to miss one another, but the knowledge that they would get married upon Skip's return in four to six weeks made them happy. Every day—every hour—was a step toward that wedding day.

CHAPTER TWENTY

Single up all lines." Captain Emerson stood on the Bridge calling the orders as they prepared to leave on this blustery chilly Monday morning. It had rained most of the night and the wind was as cold as the winter winds can sometimes be in this paradise. The dock area, the piers, and the submarines were scrubbed clean and glistening in the early morning sun that had not yet provided much warmth for the day.

"Back one-third. Rudder amidships," he said to the helmsman below in the Conning Tower. To the topside hands he barked, "Cast off all lines." He turned and ordered, "Port ahead one-third, left full rudder." He glanced over to the dock where Nance had joined some others in bidding farewell.

As they cleared the pier, he ordered, "All ahead two-thirds. Right full rudder." As they started off down the channel on their way to a destination yet unknown, Skip waved goodbye to Nance and the others on the pier. She blew him a kiss in return.

Skip turned to Curt Thomas who was at his side. "Have you and Jim Farrell gone over his computations for diving trim?"

"We sure have, Skip. I concur with his calcs. Our test dive will let us know for sure, and we can set the final trim from that dive. I'd bet a week's pay he will be within 500 pounds."

"Our waste holding tanks can cause that much variance. You guys have a good system in place with that log of everything that comes on or off, and the weights of each item. I don't know if anyone else is using that approach, but I think we should share it with SubPac one of these days."

As they left the channel and entered the Pacific Ocean, Skip turned the conn over to Curt and went below. It had become a tradition that submarine commanders who trusted their XOs let them do the test dive and set the trim on the boat. That first trim dive after being in port for a while, was always the most difficult dive the submarine would make. It was typically a slow dive, with water being pumped in transfer from one tank to another to set the ballast where it was needed. The better the calculations of weight, the easier the trim was to attain. The whole idea, of course, was that subsequent dives would take place fast and efficiently, and the balance and control of the sub would be easy to maintain.

Curt Thomas smiled at James Farrell who was at his side when they finished the trim and determined that they had only been 485 pounds off in their calculations. Having announced their corrections to the Captain, they requested permission to take her deep to check for leaks or other problems. At two hundred feet, one of the internal pipefittings on the auxiliary tank sprung a leak. A machinist had that corrected in fifteen minutes and they went to 250 feet, then 300 feet. Other than a few groans of the hull sinking under the sea pressure at this depth, there were no further leaks reported.

Curt surfaced the submarine and turned the conn over to the Officer of the Deck. They would be running on the surface throughout this day and night until the following morning when they would dive and commence their invisible operations. Topside, the storm had broken and a warm sun quickly evaporated the light cloud cover. The topside watch was pealing off the weather gear to adjust to the rapidly rising temperature. A school of dolphins broke the surface alongside the ship's hull and frolicked as though they had found a new friend. The dolphins had split into two pods along each side of the submarine where they jumped and raced for the next 45 minutes. Then, as suddenly as they appeared, they disappeared.

Transit time was boring. The submarine was in top condition. Major repairs had been made while in port. Other than a few drills that were intended to keep them on their toes, there was not much to do. Some of the men studied for promotion exams. Some worked at learning all the systems on board in preparation for earning their qualifications as submariners. Others played cards or read. A few had hobbies that did not require a lot of space, something there was little of. The mess hall was the only space available and its eight tables had to be cleared for the three meals each day.

During the nighttime, while running on the surface, the radio operators copied the Morse code signals. Other than the assigned times to receive messages from Pearl Harbor, they would copy radio transmissions of the world news. These news clippings were posted in the mess hall and were always a point of interest among the crew. Hap Henry typed the news off the code. Sometimes he would be listening to two frequencies and still seldom miss a word. The allied forces were moving through Europe. The Germans were on retreat. As the Americans joined the English and French forces from the west, the Russians were moving toward them from the east. The Axis powers had no place to go.

In the Pacific, the allied forces were making steady advances in recovering island groups the Japanese had taken early in the war. General MacArthur had landed on the beaches of Luzon and the Philippine Islands were being liberated. Guam and Okinawa had been taken back in bloody fights. One of the cooks had a map posted on the wall. Each day he updated the map showing the advances of the allied forces with colored crayons.

The men enjoyed seeing how well things were going. A lot of conversation was turning to what they were going to do after the war. The married men talked more about their families and getting back together where they had come from. The single men talked about staying in the Navy after the war. They were dedicated to the defense of their country, but had not internalized the need for that defense in the time of peace.

As was customary on these patrols, Skip Emerson reversed his sleep patterns. He slept during the daylight hours while they were making two or three knots underwater. He was up during the nighttime while they were on the surface making maximum speed and subject to detection and required evasive maneuvers. Things happened quickly when under attack and that was no time to be clearing your head from sleep. It took several days to accomplish the shift in sleep patterns, and he was never really sure his body adjusted well, but these were the hours he maintained. Actually, it was hard to tell day from night on a submarine. The watches were set in four-hour increments and there were few clues. Often the red lights were on in the Control Room during the night so that the vision of those going topside would not be impaired by going from bright lights below to no lights on deck. The red light did not constrict the pupils of the eyes as white light did. In addition, there was a twenty-four hour clock in the Control Room while others were twelve-hour clocks. The crew came to assume that if they were on the surface, it must be nighttime; if they were submerged it must be daytime.

"Man your battle stations," came the cry over the intercom followed by the electronic gong that was meant to jar anyone out of his sleep. "Chlorine gas in the After Battery Compartment. Evacuate the compartment. Close and dog the hatches."

The Captain came rushing into the Control Room followed by the XO. "What's the status, Mr. Worth?" asked the Captain.

"Sir, the medic smelled chlorine gas in the sleeping compartment. I have called General Quarters to evacuate the compartment. The hatches are secured and the Damage Control party is standing by."

"Get Chief Electrician Jeffries on the line," barked Emerson. "Chief, I want you and one of your electricians to put on the masks and go into that compartment to inspect. If we have a leak in the battery compartment, I need to know right now." Emerson knew that salt water and battery acid resulted in chlorine gas, one of the most deadly combinations that confronted submarines. The smell was the only clue to a deadly circumstance. Fortunately, they were on the surface and could suck the fumes out of that compartment with the engines running.

"Captain, this is Chief Jeffries. We are in the After Battery Room and have one man in the battery well. He reports that there is no seawater he can find in the bilges. There is no leak that we can detect. We will keep you advised as we seek out the source."

"Very well, Chief." He asked Farley Worth which cook was on duty at the time.

Second Class Cook Jackson was in the rear of the Control Room, having been evacuated from the compartment and not having another battle station to man since the cooks stood their own watch in the galley whether they were under attack or not. "I was in the galley, sir, scrubbing my pots and pans from supper."

"You are new aren't you? Where did you report from?" came the first questions of the suspicious Captain.

"Yes sir. I was on a battleship before. But I like being on this submarine."

"Were you by any chance using bleach to clean the galley?" asked the Captain.

"Oh, yes sir. I had some sticky stuff that I was cleaning. I bought some bleach over at the store when I found there was none on board."

"Get Chief Jeffries on the line. Tell him we think the culprit is the cook who used bleach in the galley. Have him check it out." He turned to Jackson, who was clearly confused. "Mr. Jackson, one of the dangers of a submarine is chlorine gas. It results from seawater getting into the batteries. It is only detected by its odor, and can kill people without even being detected. Bleach is chlorine. Your galley is located in the upper part of one of the two battery compartments. We do not allow bleach on board a submarine so that we can detect any chlorine gas by its smell. I am going to relieve Mr. Worth from his watch so he can accompany you to the galley where I want you to get rid of all the bleach you have. Do not ever bring any more on board this or any other submarine." Captain Emerson was glaring at the cook, who was visibly moved by his own fear.

"Secure from General Quarters. Turn the blowers on and evacuate the After Battery Compartment. Mr. Thomas, please make sure the Commissary Officer's instructions for getting underway call for checking for any bleach. I am confident Jackson won't make that mistake again, but we could have another new cook on another patrol."

"Aye, Captain." XO Thomas frowned at Farley who was heading aft with Cook Jackson, wondering how he had overlooked such an obvious problem in his discussions with the cooks.

Chief Jeffries reported to the Captain that the damage control team had taken the opportunity to check out both battery wells and found them free of any saltwater contamination. Emerson thanked the team and dismissed them.

Skip was sitting in the Wardroom sharing his thoughts with the XO over a cup of coffee. "Thank God that was not real. I suppose we should be glad Doc Ellis has such an acute sense of smell and knows the hazards of chlorine gas. Frankly, I don't know whether to be relieved it was only a drill, or angry that anyone could get through sub school without knowing about the prohibition on chlorine."

"I'd count it as a good drill. The crew evacuated promptly, and the damage control team performed as well as we could ask for. I'm sure that Jackson was trying to do the right thing and never thought about the ramifications of bringing bleach on board. And you can bet that neither he nor anyone else will ever forget this incident."

"I concur, XO. Let's enter it into the log as a drill so we do not have to bring any charges against Jackson. I'm sure Farley Worth will work him over till the thinks he has been judged guilty on a more serious crime than that."

Skip and Curt talked about the mission before them. They had been assigned to lifeguard patrol further north of where their last mission took place. They would be along the eastern coast of Kyushu where the water depth varied from 500 feet to 100 feet.

They would have to be extremely careful not to get in too close for too long. The enemy air cover would be greater, also. Any ships they encountered in this area would be war ships. The shipping lanes for supplies were on the interior side of these large islands, facing the China coast.

They arrived in their assigned patrol area a day ahead of schedule. Captain Emerson called for quiet time for the crew. He suggested they get all the rest they could in anticipation of getting only a little rest during the next fourteen days. He met with the officers to cover the patrol operations one last time. As each officer discussed his department's readiness, it appeared they were as ready as they could be. Engineer Farrell explained, "The timing chain on number four engine is chattering. We will replace it tonight. Beyond that, we are ready for any action. The batteries are at full power. We conducted a test discharge two nights ago, and they are fully recovered now."

"The gunnery team is likely to get a workout this time." Emerson looked all around the table as he spoke. "We are close enough to get some aircraft interference with our rescues. Once we have surfaced, we cannot dive until we have completed the rescue. We are going to minimize the surface target by keeping the decks awash where necessary. That will make rescue operations even more hazardous, but will minimize the diving time. Make sure anyone on the deck is secured by his rescue line."

The Wardroom cleared out as each officer headed out to talk with his department personnel. This might be the only chance to have a discussion without interruption until after the mission was over. It was important to the crew to feel involved in the planning for the days ahead.

CHAPTER TWENTY-ONE

R rrrip, rrrip," went the telephone in the Captain's cabin. Emerson grabbed for it immediately. "Captain here," he said.

"Captain, this is Henry in the Radio Shack. We have just received an urgent message from Carrier Air Group 6. They have a fighter wing that has been heavily hit. At least three of their planes are going to have to ditch in our vicinity."

"Very well," responded Emerson as he slid into his shoes and headed toward the Control Room. A glance at his watch told him it was 0430. The planes were obviously part of a night strike. The enemy seemed to be getting better at tracking the aircraft, even at night.

"What is our position?" he asked the Watch Chief who was standing in the Control Room.

"We are on the surface making turns for ten knots, heading 270 true."

As he headed up through the Conning Tower to the Bridge, he hollered, "Captain coming up. What is our position?"

"We are heading 270 at ten knots under clear skies and stage one sea. Radio has informed me of the urgent message, Sir. We are heading in the direction the aircraft should be coming from."

"Good move. That will save us some time. Call for the rescue party and gun detail to assemble in the Forward Torpedo Room." Emerson looked all around to assure himself that he knew what their status was. He could hear the rumble of the exhaust from the two engines that were on line.

"Bring on the other two engines," he ordered. "Captain has the Conn. Ask Mr. Thomas to come to the Conning Tower."

"Captain, this is the XO. We have the plot ready for splash down. We can track from here unless we are forced under."

"We are not going to dive until we have the rescue completed. I am going to put the gunnery detail on the forward gun and pray that we have some time. It looks like there may be two or three aircraft involved in ditching in the same area. If we get lucky, perhaps they will pick the same spot.

"Air lookouts, keep a keen eye for aircraft coming in. As soon as they hit the sea, turn them over to the sea lookouts and retrain your eyes on the skies. We are likely to get some enemy aircraft out of the land mass on the horizon trying to keep us from the rescue."

"Captain, I have two aircraft at two o'clock off the starboard quarter. Looks like they are on fire and heading in to the sea. I see a parachute now. No, I see two parachutes in the air. Same direction."

"Well done. Keep a lookout for the third aircraft. I've got the two parachutes in my vision." Emerson turned to the PA and called for the gunnery detail and rescue team to use the forward hatch.

"All ahead full. Steer 280." He heard the responses from the Conning Tower and felt the surge of the four engines powering the motors at full thrust. The forward hatch popped open and the men came scrambling topside. The gun detail raced to the five-inch gun and started the loading procedure. The rescue team was getting the inflatable boat out from under the decking and preparing to take it over the side if necessary. They would not inflate the boat until the last minute. That way, if it were not needed, they would not have to take the time to collapse it or lose it if the sub were under attack. They tied it down midway between the hatch and the gun to keep it out of the way for both details. The chiefs of both details raised their hands in salute to indicate they were ready. Emerson acknowledged each with a return salute.

The same lookout who had reported the first two parachutes called out, "Captain, I see another parachute in the air, same bearing as the first two, but further away."

"Captain," the XO called up to the Bridge, "We have the first two aviators spotted on the large scope at 2000 yards dead ahead. The third parachute just hit the water, five degrees to starboard and out another 1500yards. Suggest we continue on course another four minutes before commencing recovery operations."

"Very well, XO," responded Emerson. "Set the timer and let me know at three minutes, forty-five seconds." The Captain searched around the sky. So far there were no indications of other aircraft. "Keep a sharp lookout in the air, now. I expect some company at any time."

As they approached the spot where the aviators hit the water as marked by the floating parachutes, the Captain called for reducing speed to two knots and executed their recovery maneuver. As soon as the engines backed off, the rescue crew went to action. Within ten minutes, both aviators were on board and being escorted below while the sub headed for the spot the third flyer had landed.

It was another ten minutes before they approached the area. The aviator had not been so lucky as his two colleagues. He was unconscious and still attached to his parachute, and was being pulled along by the tide. Fortunately, his 'Mae West' kept his face out of the water and he didn't drown. One of the seamen dove off the tank top and released the flyer's parachute after attaching a line to him. They were both towed back to the sub and up out of the water. Two seamen grabbed the aviator and slid him down the ladder into the Forward Torpedo Room. The rescue detail was secured, and the gunnery detail unloaded their gun and put the plug back into the barrel. The Captain felt much better as he saw the hatch close and knew they could not dive if they needed to.

There was still no indication of any surface or air contacts, so the Captain decided they would stay on the surface another hour. He reinstated the watch detail and went below, thanking the XO and crew in the Conning Tower on his way down. Thomas followed him down the ladder and they headed forward to greet their new wards.

The Forward Torpedo Room was full of activity. Chief Bill Edwards and his rescue detail had gotten the three pilots into dry clothing and coffee was being served. Doc Ellis had attended to the medical needs as best he could. The first pilot they picked up has some minor burns on his legs from a cockpit fire he had been unable to fully extinguish. The third pilot had a sprained left wrist where he hit the canopy to jar it open so he could bail out. Doc had dressed the burns and wrapped the sprained wrist.

"Welcome aboard, gentlemen." Greeted Emerson. "I'm Lieutenant Commander Charles Emerson, the Captain of the U.S.S. Snook. This is Lieutenant Curt Thomas, the Executive Officer. We are pleased to have you on board. We are currently sailing on the surface, monitoring the distress frequencies in case any of your fellow pilots has trouble getting back to the aircraft carrier. We will be diving at dawn or if any enemy airplanes are spotted, to ensure the enemy does not become aware of our presence."

"Captain, I am Lieutenant Glenn Smith, a fighter pilot from the Forrestal. I Can't tell you how happy I was to see your ship rising out of the water. It is an eerie feeling to parachute out of your plane into a sea where there is no ship in sight. It does not give one a secure feeling. So when this huge black hull appeared on the surface, I felt a thrill that I would not have thought possible, realizing that you had been down in the water listening for us all the time."

"Actually, we were on the surface. It's just that we blend into the sea so well we are often not seen." Emerson wanted to clarify the issue for all the pilots.

"Captain, I want to thank you also. I am Lt. J.G. Homer Jenkins. I echo Glenn's comments. I got burned waiting too long in the cockpit of my plane. Not seeing you out there made me want to stay with my plane as long as I could. My question is, how long will we be on your submarine and what will you do with us?"

"We must stay on station in this area for the next three days. Then we will arrange a transfer to one of the Forrestal's support ships to get you back to your squadron." Skip explained they would be staying here where bunks were available for them. The Wardroom was immediately aft of this compartment. They would have their meals in the Wardroom and could use it for casual purposes. The Captain offered them the run of the ship but asked that they spend their time forward. In case of any emergency, or if the ship went to battle stations, they were assigned to the Wardroom to keep them out of the way.

Lt. J.G. Trent was the last airman to speak. "Thanks for picking me up, too. And thanks to Doc for bandaging this wrist of mine. I thought sure I had broken it, hammering my way out of my plane. What a time for the canopy to stick. I especially want to thank Bruce for jumping into the water to save me. I guess I blacked out on my way down after I jumped and pulled the parachute ripcord. Thank God for the 'Mae West' or I would have drowned before you got to me."

"We are happy to have picked up all three of you," responded Curt Thomas. "This is not a hotel, but you will find that we are dedicated to our task of providing lifeguard services. And you will find that our food is much better than any you have had on any surface ships. Once we have commenced our daytime operations, underwater, I will arrange a tour of the boat so you can see what we are all about. Until then, I suggest that you rest. After your ordeal, I would think you might need some rest. If you need anything, just ask. Chief Edwards and his crew are right here. The Captain and I are not very far away. We want you to be comfortable on board."

Skip and Curt left the compartment and stopped in the Wardroom for a cup of coffee and a debriefing on the rescue. They discussed the doubling of the lookouts and decided that it was necessary to have at least two watching the skies as the other two watched the surface and maintained visual contact with the aviators in the sea. Both were concerned about the number of men topside, in case of attack, but could not figure out how to operate without any of them. Each man had a reason to be topside during the rescue. The gunnery detail was minimal to operate the five-inch canon and the aerial machine gun.

The key, they decided, was to continue to drill the men on quickly securing the topside and getting below in case of attack. The gunnery detail was intended to be a defensive maneuver, to be used to allow the rescue detail to get below. Then they would dive and evade the enemy.

At first sign of dawn, the Captain ordered the dive. Once their trim was set and they were at periscope depth, the floating whip antenna was deployed and the radio receivers were transferred to that antenna. Hap Henry had trained several interested crewmembers, and all the officers, on the operations of the emergency frequency radio equipment. The

Radio Shack became a popular place and it was not unusual to find several off-duty crewmembers hanging around at any time. It was a cramped little space and the XO needed to be able to get in on a moments notice.

Curt and Hap decided the solution was to pipe the radio frequency into the crew's mess area where the men could sit and listen and where someone was always present. The idea worked. The crew felt they were involved in listening for any emergency calls and the Radio Shack was once again available for the sensitive messages that were sent and received there.

Other than the test messages that were received on the hour, the radio was quiet for most of the day. One emergency call was received in the late afternoon, but the plane was far to the south of their assigned area and they ignored the call knowing that another submarine or surface ship would pick up that call. The last rays of sunlight were staining the western sky with a deep purple hue when the received a call to action.

A bomber squadron out of Okinawa had run into heavy flak and been unable to drop their bombs over their assigned targets. They headed out to sea to make a run from the east when one of the planes developed engine trouble. They were going to have to ditch the aircraft.

The Captain and XO manned the two periscopes as the submarine headed for the bearings that were radioed from the aircraft. They were within 30 miles of that position and the aircraft was headed toward them. At a top speed of 10 knots, they would quickly use up the reserve in their batteries, a dangerous procedure if they were attacked and had to dive before the batteries could be charged. Emerson called for turns of six knots. He hoped they would be able to see the bomber as it came down. Both he and Thomas doubted the aviators could hang on till sunset.

The rescue detail had been assembled forward. The gunnery detail was standing by to precede them topside. The rest of the crew was at battle stations.

"Surface, surface, surface," Emerson called over the public address system. The klaxon sounded three times, and the Diving Officer took action to blow the tanks and use the bow and stern planes to get them on the surface as quickly as possible. Skip Emerson climbed the ladder and undogged the hatch to the Bridge as soon as the Diving Officer's calls indicated the shears were out of the water. As the Captain took a quick look around, he called for the lookouts and rescue details. Thomas had kept a constant scan around the sub through the periscope that he continued till the lookouts were topside. Then he moved to the plotting board to lead the team who would track the aviators once they were spotted, until they were picked up.

The pilot of the bomber decided he had enough power to crash-land the plane in the sea rather than have the crew bail out. He dumped his bombs and the fuel that would have gotten them back to base. He and the copilot looked for the rescue ship but didn't see anything. He hoped that their emergency call had been received. The nose and tail gunners, and the bombardier, assembled with the belly gunners. They broke out the inflatable boat and laid it on the deck so it could be pushed through the hatch and inflated as soon as they came to rest. The pilot and copilot held the steering yokes firmly as they reduced speed and turned into the wind to give them maximum lift. They had talked about this procedure ever since flight school, but this time it was real. Their flaps extended, they brought their lumbering, heavy aircraft toward the sea. At the last moment, they lifted the nose and gunned the throttles. The plane started to lift, then stalled, then pancaked into the water.

There was a mad scramble for the bomber's hatch. The first crewmembers out pulled the lifeboat onto the wing, pulled the inflators and pushed it into the sea. As they jumped towards it, the remaining crewmembers emerged onto the wing and jumped out toward the boat. Already, the bomber was settling down into the water. The four gunners were paddling feverishly to get the lifeboat away from the body of the bomber so they would not be sucked down with the vortex created when the aircraft sunk.

U.S.S. Snook was making almost 21 knots, racing for the site of the splashdown. The lookouts, expecting to see a mass of parachutes, almost missed the big lumbering aircraft as it crash-landed. At first they thought it was an enemy plane flying low to the water. Then they realized it was the bomber seeking rescue. The pilot had decided to set it in the sea hoping an easy crash would give them more time to evacuate before the plane sank.

The aircraft had come to rest about 10 miles from where the rescuers were. At this speed, it would take about twenty-five minutes to arrive at the scene. Captain Emerson warned the lookouts to keep a vigilant watch for aircraft or ships. They still had some twilight before the final darkness of the moonless night set in. Skip had secured the periscope watch and lowered the periscopes to keep their silhouette as low as possible for ships over the horizon. He wanted to be sure they would see the enemy before being seen.

The airmen huddled in the lifeboat. They prayed for a friendly ship to arrive before the enemy found them. The tail gunner had suffered a few scratches on his left arm crawling through the tube from the tail to the belly of the bomber. It was nothing to be concerned about as long as they were not in the water. The men feared any scent of blood in the water might attract sharks. As the four gunners rowed, the three officers searched around for any signs of rescue craft.

Then they heard it. The sound of an airplane was distinct and familiar to the airmen. It was a multiengine plane, coming out of the mainland. It's intent was not rescue, but destruction. It started its long run toward them. The pilot ordered everybody out of the lifeboat. They would be safer, he said, hanging on to the outside of the boat as it became a target for the Jenny bomber, the familiar enemy aircraft that patrolled these areas. As it drew nearer, the airmen realized they were not the target. The Jenny was heading towards something in the water they had not seen. A larger, more ominous target was bearing down towards them. It was a submarine on the surface, some four or five miles away.

The gunnery detail was standing by awaiting orders to commence firing. Skip Emerson was waiting until the aircraft committed its dive towards them. It might get careless if it thought they had no topside guns. At the very least, Skip hoped their return of fire would distract the bomber from any direct attack on them. He was not diving until the airmen were safely on board.

"Commence firing," he called out. "Steer 20 degrees to port." He wanted to head toward the enemy aircraft to give the smallest target possible. The machine gun started chattering immediately before any shots were fired toward them. The Jenny leaned in its turn just as the five-inch gun belched its shell toward the plane. This pass over the submarine had been intended as a quick look before the strike attack commenced. The plane was taken off guard when the sub started firing at it. Its belly was exposed to the Snook's machine gun as the plane banked away. The heavy five-inch shell missed but the machine gun strafed the fuselage. The enemy returned fire but was off target.

The Captain changed their course to put the sub between the enemy aircraft and the lifeboat. He maintained speed so that he could keep evasive maneuvers at their peek. The lifeboat was within a mile of them now. He would have to slow the sub after the next attack run of the Jenny. As the plane turned and headed back toward them, Emerson realized form its altitude that it was intending to release a torpedo.

"Left full rudder," he screamed. "All stop." The Jenny had used his course and speed as its lead. It was unable to adjust before the torpedo dropped from its underside. The torpedo went screaming across the bow at a point where they would have been had Skip not changed their course and speed.

The machine gun put as many shells in the air as it could, forcing the aircraft to change its course from swinging towards their new position. The five-inch gun got lucky. With only the aircraft movement to compute, it hit the right wing and tore it off. The plane was in its dive mode and could not pull out. It hit the water some two miles to the west and exploded in a ball of fire.

Captain Emerson gave a thumbs up to the crew manning the five-inch gun. He then called for the rescue detail to standby for pickup. As he maneuvered the sub toward the lifeboat he could see the cheering of the airmen who had witnessed the event. In the next ten minutes they were aboard, the topside detail secured, and all extra personnel were sent below. The last rays of light were vanishing to the west as the submarine turned back in the direction from which it had come. The Captain turned the watch over to the Duty Officer with a warning that more enemy planes might follow the one they had shot down. His instructions were to dive if there was any doubt about what to do.

Skip Emerson dropped into the Conning Tower, picked up the microphone to the 1MC and addressed the crew. "Gentlemen, this is your Captain speaking. I congratulate each of you on your continued success. We have proven our skills in the face of adversity. We now have seven additional airmen on board. In the course of this rescue, a Japanese Jenny bomber tried to torpedo us. We not only evaded her torpedo, but also shot her down. The combination of machine gun strafing and heavy five-inch gun did the job for us. I am very proud of each of you."

Skip went forward to greet the seven airmen and to see that everything was secured from the rescue detail. As usual, Chief Edwards had briefed the new airmen on living conditions on a submarine. Emerson added his caveats.

"Captain, on behalf of my crew, I want to thank you," said Major Denning, the pilot of the bomber. "What a magnificent show you put on for us. At first, we thought no one was going to rescue us. Then, when that Jenny came out of the sky, we thought it was heading for us. And then we were treated to a show of Naval gunfire and maneuvers that we will never forget. This is all so very different than what we were expecting. Needless to say, we are all glad to be here."

"We hope that your stay will be a pleasant one. We are supposed to transfer out Naval airmen to a surface ship tomorrow. You will be transferred to that same ship and they will make arrangements to get you back to your base. On behalf of our crew, we welcome you aboard the U.S.S. Snook."

CHAPTER TWENTY-TWO

The news of success travels fast. The U.S.S. Snook had rescued seventeen airmen so far. They had shot down a large enemy bomber in the process. They had shown the way for other submarines to be involved through a major communications breakthrough. The press on the islands had picked up the stories from Submarine Pacific Headquarters. The news services quickly spread the stories to the mainland. Snook was a popular name among all fliers and their families.

Commander James Walker, the Public Information Officer for ComSubPac was doing his job. It was important to remind the public of the important job that the submarines were doing. Most of their patrols were classified. These rescues were going to be made public by the aviators whose lives were saved. Better, he decided, that they get some credit for breaking the stories to the press.

Walker sat in Captain Brannigan's office, strategizing on the next steps to take. A large reception for Skip Emerson and his crew was in order upon their return. The engagement of Emerson to a Navy nurse would also add to the excitement of their return. The whole world could share in this romantic sea adventure. Phil Brannigan said he had talked to Admiral Pennington about promoting Emerson to full Commander, but did not want Jim Walker to publish that news. It was not appropriate to preempt the old man, in what would become added publicity at the right time.

"We have all the pieces for a major awards dinner for the crew after the reception. The Air Force has indicated that it wants to give Bronze Medals to each officer on the boat, and their Distinguished Service Cross to the skipper. I'd like to call Miss Jones about their engagement and wedding plans."

"I think we have more than enough to fill a couple of weeks and keep that momentum growing, Phil. Thanks for your support on this. If you can nudge the old man on the promotion, that will be the highlight for all the other submarine commanders who are looking for ways to get themselves promoted."

Commander Walker went out of Captain Brannigan's office and turned down the stairs, full of the kind of excitement that warmed any old city editor's heart. Always looking for a way to promote the submarine force, Jim was happy about this turn of events. It had been a long time since he had been able to publish any of their successes. When he got back to his office, he asked his clerk to place a call to Tripler Hospital, to a Miss Nancy Jones, a Navy nurse stationed there.

"Lieutenant Jones, this is Commander Walker from SubPac calling with good news."

"Oh?" replied Nance. "What is that, Commander?"

"Have you seen the story about the Snook in the local press? This morning's edition of the Breeze tells about their rescue of seventeen airmen. We are planning to do a series of stories building up to their return in a couple of weeks. We would like to personalize some of the press, if you will let us."

"Sure, how can I help?"

"We have heard that Lt. Cdr. Emerson and you were engaged before he left for this patrol and that you are planning a marriage when he returns. We would like your permission to highlight the stories with some of this information."

"Well, that sounds good to me. Can you do that and still keep the focus on Skip and his crew? They deserve all the attention."

"Leave it to me, Miss Jones. May I call you Nancy?"

"Sure. You can call me Nance if you wish. That is what my friends call me."

"And you may call me Jim, if you wish. I will need to meet with you to get some of the particulars on your engagement and wedding plans. I would also like a picture or two. Do you have anything of the two of you? That would be great with the engagement news."

"I'd be happy to meet with you, Jim. Just name the time and place. I've been working double shifts to keep busy, and to build up some leave time for when Skip returns. Do you think that will be in two weeks?"

"There have been no extensions from our end, so we think they will be back as planned. How about lunch one day this week? I can pick you up and we will go somewhere that you enjoy, for a leisurely lunch. It sounds like you may be overdue for a break anyway. My wife and I remember those days when I was at sea. Just when I start thinking about 'the good old days,' I remember what was not so good about those days. We hated the separation and I'm thankful that I got this office job so we are together every day. Marlene is here in Honolulu with me. We decided not to send her back to the mainland after the attack on Pearl. In spite of the danger, we could not bear to be apart any more."

They agreed to meet Wednesday noon. Jim Walker hung up the telephone feeling that this was going to be a good series of stories. Nance Jones was just the kind of person who would tug at the heartstrings of America.

Later that day both the AP and UPI bureau chiefs called Walker wanting to get additional information on the local news story. They were both interested in the Commander's idea of a series of articles building up to the return of the U.S.S. Snook. This would be hot news for their wire services. Jim Walker knew that taking the bureau chiefs into his confidence was the right thing to do. Unlike the local press that often had to be spoon-fed with stories, the Associated Press and United Press International were top caliber journalists.

In fact, the AP bureau chief had already talked with the Air Force to corroborate the rescue of the bomber aviators and had gotten some terrific quotes. One of the rescued fighter pilots reported the awesome sight of the submarine surfacing, coming at a time when he thought he had been abandoned. One of the bomber aviators reported that the food on the submarine was so good he was thinking about signing up with the

Navy next time. The bomber pilot told about the Japanese plane that was coming in to strafe their lifeboat when it was drawn off by the submarine and then shot down by the sub's deck guns.

Commander Walker added these notes to his file. He then placed a call to the Navy Carrier Air Group staff offices on Ford Island to see if they could add any quotes from Navy airmen rescued by the Snook. By the end of Tuesday, Walker had a complete outline for the series of articles and had completed writing the first three. He would wait to finish the others until after he met with Nance Jones, the young nurse whom he would portray as giving her career to the Navy to be part of the war effort, and who had met and fallen in love with a Navy warrior, the commanding officer of the U.S.S. Snook. Jim liked the spin he was developing for Nurse Jones's part in the series.

Walker would like to have paid credit to Curt Thomas and the radioman who designed and tested the new antenna system being fitted on several other submarines after being proven on the Snook. He knew, however, that such classified information could not be shared at this time. He would work up some material on the use of deck guns now that the AP was going to quote the pilot of the downed bomber. It was important that the glory be shared by as many of the crew as possible. This was not just about Lt. Cdr. Emerson. It was about the U.S. submarines fighting in the Pacific. Submarines were doing unusual tasks to speed the end of the war.

Much of what they were doing was part of their role as "the silent service" and would not be revealed for years to come. It was, therefore, important to chronicle what they could to let the public know they were a vital power in the war. Snook would become a symbol of everything submarines stood for. The task Jim Walker saw for himself was the development of that symbolism.

The luncheon with Lt. Jones went well. Nance was a beauty, as well as being personable. Jim decided that any personal appearances she might do would only enhance their image. She brought some photographs of Skip and her at a formal tea, as well as some casual shots at a luau. Jim promised to get them back to her. They discussed her background and early family life. Jim asked if Nance thought she would make a good Navy wife.

"I feel as though I am already. I find that when Skip is in port, our lives are built around his schedule. I make as much time available to him as he wants. That includes the obligatory social events, or 'command performances' as the wives seem to call them. Actually, we are private people who prefer to keep to ourselves as much as we can. When Skip is at sea, I work extra shifts to keep busy and to keep my mind occupied with positive thoughts. Sometimes, though, I get really scared thinking about what Skip and his crew are going through."

"We have all been through tough times," Walker responded. "Let me give you our home telephone number. My wife, Marlene, would enjoy a call from you. She has been through some of the same times you are going through now. Perhaps it would be helpful for you to have someone to talk with."

Nance thanked Jim and put the card in her purse. She appreciated the gesture. "In addition to the series of news articles, we are planning a large reception for the crew when they return. It will start with the Admiral being on hand at the pier to greet your fiancé and his crew. Then we are putting together a formal reception for the officers at our headquarters, followed by a reception for the entire crew at the Sub Base club. There will be awards presented and as much glitter as we can put together, spread over several days. We want you to be a special part of all this."

They finished their lunches and Walker returned Nance to the hospital. He asked her to keep in touch and promised to let her know if he heard anything further about the arrival of the Snook. As Nance walked back toward her ward, she decided there were a lot of good people in the world, all trying to make it a better place in which to live.

CHAPTER TWENTY-THREE

Radio traffic had been constant all morning. The Snook was in the northern part of its operating area where the British forces had joined in the allied strikes. The Brits were flying DeHaviland dive-bombers with a crew of two. The pilot fired the forward wing mounted guns and controlled the release of the bomb strapped under the fuselage. The second crewmember was a gunner who faced aft and protected their rear quarters and sides from his bubble-enclosed machine gun turret. These airmen flew off the smaller British aircraft carriers and had less range of flight than their American counterparts. Yet they were committed to doing their part in the victory over Japan.

Skip Emerson and his crew had made three rescues on the prior day, picking up six airmen out of the water. Each rescue had been completed within ninety minutes of the radio message being received. In spite of the calm seas and bright sunlight, no enemy planes interfered with the rescue missions. The lookouts had to be constantly reminded not to drop their vigilance. A submarine was vulnerable on the surface. They must not forget that for a minute.

They were running slowly at periscope depth with their floating antenna deployed. Radioman Henry was intent on monitoring the emergency frequencies. XO Thomas was sitting in the Radio Shack reading the news received during the nightly broadcast. He was pleased with what he read. The allied forces were making progress. The submarine forces had literally cut off the supply lines and the combined air forces were striking hard on the Japanese soil. The Japanese fleet had been resoundly defeated at Midway, and what was left had retreated.

Curt was anxious to get his command, but was more anxious for the war to end. He decided that many of the submarine skippers would retire their commissions after the war and he would be ready to step into one of the commands. Most of these men were going home to their families and jobs. He had decided the Navy was his career. He had no family to be concerned about on these long voyages.

"Did you hear that, Sir?" said Henry. "They are calling for us to rescue another one. I've got the coordinates written down here."

Thomas was jarred out of his daydream by Henry's voice. "No. I missed it. Glad that you were alert, Hap. Give me the coordinates and we will start our search."

"Captain," he said over the telephone, "We have just received another call for help. I'll be in the Conning Tower working out the coordinates and heading us toward the target area."

"Very well, XO. I'll meet you there in a couple of minutes." Emerson pulled his pants on and slipped into his shoes. He had been dozing on his bunk when the telephone rang.

"This one is ditching about twenty miles west of our position. We have come about and are ready to surface on you command, Captain. Our search indicates clear skies."

"Surface, surface, surface," called the Captain through the 1MC. "Rescue and gunnery detail to the Forward Torpedo Room. All others man your battle stations."

As he climbed onto the Bridge, he scanned the horizon quickly, then called for the lookouts waiting in the Conning Tower to come up. He called for flank speed. They were about forty-five minutes from the target area if the enemy aircraft would leave them alone. They would not see the Brits splash down from this distance, making the siting more difficult. And the Brits would not see them coming to the rescue until the sub was almost upon them.

"Enemy aircraft on the horizon off the port bow," cried the port lookout.

"Dive, dive," commanded the Captain after he ordered the lookouts to clear the Bridge. As he slammed the deck hatch, he ordered full speed, 100 feet, full planes and right full rudder. The forward speed put them quickly under the water. Standing in the Conning Tower Emerson counted the twenty seconds he believed should put the aircraft over head.

"Bring her up to periscope depth," he ordered. A quick search found the enemy aircraft still heading away on its bearing. It appeared the plane had not seen them or the airmen.

"Surface, surface, surface. Now stand by for a crash dive." Emerson warned the crew they might be heading right back down if the plane returned. The skies were clear as he scanned around. He called the lookouts up and turned the sub toward the target area, once again laying on flank speed. They were still twenty minutes from their destination, but he hoped to pick up some indication of the airmen soon.

"Flare off the starboard beam, Sir," called the starboard lookout.

"I've got it," Emerson responded. The Captain changed their heading and called the rescue and gunnery details topside.

Thomas appeared at his side. "Hope no one else saw that flare," he said. "I told the rescue detail we are trying to set a record with this recovery. We are a little too close to that plane siting to feel comfortable out here."

"You are right. The sooner we get back under water, the better I will feel. I'm not sure how long it would have taken us to find the airmen if they had not fired the flare, though." Then Captain admonished the lookouts to keep a constant search for aircraft.

As the submarine neared the airmen, the rescue team went into action. Two men were on top of the port tank tops ready to cast their lines into the water. The submarine was slowing and the port side would be the sheltered side from the wave action. The other members of the rescue team were holding the lines fastened to the crew on the tank tops and to the lines that would be passed over to the airmen. Fortunately, the airmen had tied themselves together so a common pickup could be made. This would save valuable minutes in the rescue.

"Aircraft on the horizon. Off the starboard beam," shouted a lookout.

"Gunnery detail, look alive," ordered the Captain. The sub was dead in the water. This was the worst possible moment for attack. "Let's get those men on board and below."

The plane was skimming the surface and almost upon the submarine before it saw its target. It screamed overhead at no more than one hundred feet before it could even fire a round. The sub's fifty millimeter anti aircraft gun barked and the five-inch cannon boomed as the gunnery detail hoped for a lucky shot. The plane banked and turned back toward the submarine. This pass would not be without gunfire.

One airman was aboard and the other, an injured man, was being hauled up the side as the plane made its second pass. "Give them everything you have," called the Skipper, "Then get below. We are going to crash dive right after the plane passes us." He had already called for full speed and was turning the sub toward the plane to make the smallest target possible. They would need some headway speed to help them dive, too.

The dive-bomber dropped a torpedo as it commenced its run at the submarine. It was clear to Captain Emerson that the torpedo was off its target and would run down their starboard side as long as he did not turn into it. The deck guns opened fire just as the strafing emitted from the plane. One of the gunners received a direct hit, and one of the rescue detail caught a ricocheting shell on his hand, as he was the last one down the forward hatch. The gunnery detail dragged their colleague toward the forward hatch even as the Captain was clearing the Bridge. Emerson watched the forward hatch close before he called for the dive and slid down the ladder into the Conning Tower. Barking out orders for course, speed and depth, he continued down into the Control Room.

They were approaching 250 feet on a ninety-degree down glide when they heard the depth charges above and behind them. Fortunately, the enemy was misinformed about the depths to which the newer submarines could venture and often set their charges to go off above 150 feet. This aircraft had done all the damage it was going to do, but would probably mark the area with die and call for surface ships to come in and continue the search.

Knowing they had to vacate the area, Captain Emerson reduced speed and turned eastward. He gave the Diving Officer orders to proceed for one hour at 250 feet before coming back up to periscope depth. They would continue moving in this direction till nightfall. Hopefully they could then surface and rendezvous with a British ship for transfer of the airmen. It might also be necessary to transfer the crewmen that had been injured if his medic couldn't attend to the medical needs.

By the time Captain Emerson arrived in the Forward Torpedo Room, the new airmen had been introduced to the rescue detail that pulled them from the sea. They had put on dry clothing and were being treated to a cup of hot soup.

Doc Ellis was working on the gunner who had received the direct hit. He was still unconscious and it did not look good. The chest wound needed medical attention that was beyond the Doc's abilities. He would make the man as comfortable as possible and keep him anesthetized with morphine, but the seaman would need to get to a hospital to get the surgical attention he needed.

The other seaman, who was hit as he was going down the ladder, had received only a flesh wound. His arm was bandaged and was going to be O.K. He would get his 'purple heart' award without suffering too much. He was alert and laughing at the jokes his buddies were making. Doc Ellis was sure that he would be back on his feet in a day or two.

Skip Emerson congratulated both the rescue detail and the gunnery detail on another fine job. The rescue detail had set a new record in getting the airmen out of the water and below decks. They were all mindful that the gunners' defensive work had caused the plane to miss its target badly. The torpedo had been released too soon and the plane had moved defensively causing its guns to miss their targets. There could have been far more damage done. The gunners were fussing about having missed their chance at shooting down another plane. They listened to their skipper explain how important it was that they all got away without damage to the submarine. Now they felt better about the job they had done.

Skip stopped in the Wardroom to rest his weary bones. "Well, Curt, we can add eight more airmen to our rescue numbers. Unfortunately, we will need to transfer Seaman Jacobs with the airmen so he can get proper medical treatment. His wounds are deep and beyond Doc Ellis' abilities."

"We are damn lucky," the XO said, "that plane didn't do a lot more damage than it did. That was cool thinking on your part to turn toward the plane, or they would have gotten us broadside with their torpedo. As it was, their strafing was off target or we could have suffered a lot more personal injuries too."

"I think we can thank our gunnery detail for that. The pilot was unsure of himself and not willing to risk coming directly at us for very long. I was really concerned for our lookouts that are so unprotected up in the periscope shears. Again, the gunners distracted the plane into a defensive mode long enough for us to get away."

"Do you think that we will have more problems with enemy planes today, Skip?"

"They will be looking for us, I'm sure. We will just keep our heads down for most of the day. Any surface ships sent our way will only be able to determine that we are not still in the contact area. They won't know which way we have gone or how far. I think we will be safe to continue on our track. As evening sets in, we will stick up our antenna and have Hap Henry activate the low powered transmitter to make contact with the Brits so we can arrange the transfer. In the meantime, I'm going to catch some sleep. The adrenalin has finally stopped flowing and I'm bushed."

"I'm going to walk through the boat and then I, too, am going to catch some sleep so I will be alert for tonight. I will let the Diving Officer know where he can find either of us."

The day was extremely quiet. The Diving Officer followed the orders for depth change, but otherwise the submarine slipped though the water at four knots, heading 090 on the compass. Every two hours, the XO would raise the periscope and take a quick look around. After lowering it, he would check their position on the charts.

Two watch shifts went by without any interruptions in their routine sailing. Shortly after the Engineering Officer had taken over the dive, the Captain came into the Control Room and asked the status of the boat. Farrell reported their position, course, speed and depth. He also told the

Captain their trim status. They had about four more hours left before they would need a battery charge.

Skip thanked Jim Farrell for the status report and told him what they would be doing that evening. He then headed aft for a quick walkthrough of the boat. He stopped by the Radio Shack and asked the duty radioman to call Hap Henry to meet with the XO and him in fifteen minutes.

CHAPTER TWENTY-FOUR

s dusk set upon the sea, the Snook once again came up to periscope depth. XO Thomas conducted an extended visual search of the surface and the air. "Everything looks clear up here, Captain," he said to Emerson who was sitting in the Radio Shack with Hap Henry.

"Very well, XO. Take her up till the decks are awash. Then we will energize the low power transmitter and see if we can make contact with the Brits." Emerson gave the special frequency to Henry who dialed it into the transmitter, while the XO brought the sub up to 35 feet.

"Captain, the shears are clear," came the message from XO Thomas, indicating that the periscope shears and mastheads were above the waterline.

"I'm ready when you are, Sir," said Hap Henry.

"Very well, let's do it," replied the Captain. "Keep your transmissions as brief as possible. Even with the low power, we are radiating so that we can be heard out there by anyone within 50 miles. If it is the enemy, we don't want to give them enough time to home in on their direction finder."

"Brit One, Brit One, this is Life Guard One. Over." Henry snapped his finger off the transmitter key.

They waited for a response. It was absolutely silent in the Radio Shack. Both Emerson and Henry listened intently for a signal. The seconds dragged by. Henry checked his switches to confirm that everything was set up correctly. With the Captain's permission, he ran a test signal through the receiver to make sure it was functioning properly. At the end of two minutes of silence, Emerson ordered Henry to transmit again.

"Brit One, Brit One, this is Life Guard One. Over."

"Life Guard One," a faint voice was heard. "We copy you. We are proceeding under full power to pickup point Able Baker. Over."

"Roger. Out." Hap turned off the transmitter. They had kept their transmission time to a minimum. The pickup point had been designated in the operating instructions. There was no need for further communications unless the submarine could not get to the agreed upon pickup point. Since Snook was within five miles of that point, they would await the British greyhound.

"Mr. Thomas," called the Captain to the XO, "Take us back down to periscope depth and set a periscope watch for the British ship. Their faint signal suggests they are about 50 miles out, so we can expect them in a couple of hours. We will stay here until we confirm their arrival on station."

"Well done, Hap." Emerson shook the radioman's hand. The Captain then left the Radio Shack and went into the forward part of the Control Room to thank the crew for their part in the communications contact, and to brief them on what was next. He knew that the rest of the crew was anxious about the task at hand. "Now hear this. This is your Captain speaking. We have just made contact with a British ship that is coming to pick up the airmen and Seaman Jacobs. They will arrive in approximately two hours. At that time we will surface for the transfer. The rescue detail and gunnery detail will accomplish that transfer once we are surfaced. Thank you for your fine performance. I am proud to serve with each of you."

The mood of the crew was one of excitement. They were proud of their accomplishments. They had set a record in their prior rescues. And now they were adding eight additional rescues to the total number. There was sure to be some kind of recognition when they returned to Pearl Harbor at the end of this patrol. The ship's cook, who had the evening watch, was preparing pastries for the next day. He decided that this event warranted special treatment. He asked Lt. Farley Worth to pass the word that the mess hall was open for all and that there were pies and pastries to celebrate the occasion.

The full moon shone like a beacon from above, breaking into a thousand shimmering spheres on the slight chop of the sea. The XO and the Quartermaster took turns manning the periscope. It had been two hours and fifteen minutes since the Captain had made contact with the British ship. Each of them had checked the star positions twice during this interval to make sure they were where they said they would be. They expected the Brits to run without any navigational lights, so they did not expect to make visual contact until the ship was close at hand. Nonetheless, they were still nervous in their anticipation.

Captain Emerson had joined them fifteen minutes ago and was a calming influence on them. He reminded them that the British ship that had received their communications would have to communicate with the flagship of their flotilla for a decision on who would make the pickup. All of this would add to the time needed to get to the transfer location.

"I have something on the big scope," said the Quartermaster. "All I can make out is a disruption of the moon shining on the surface. It's like a big black hole out there."

"Let's wait until we can see a profile before we surface. They still have a ways to go." The Captain turned away from his scope. He called down through the hatch to the Diving Officer, "Have the rescue and gunnery details assembled in the Forward Torpedo Room. We will be ready to transfer soon."

As the frigate slowed and turned, the silhouette revealed it to be British in design. The gun turret placements and the rake of the smoke stack were unmistakable. The Captain ordered the submarine to the surface. With no forward motion, the Snook came straight up out of the water at a distance of some two hundred yards off the side of the frigate.

While Snook' gunnery and rescue details were scrambling onto the deck, the Captain stood on the Bridge holding a bullhorn. The British ship maneuvered to a position about 50 yards to the side of the submarine and put a boat into the water.

Skip Emerson put the bullhorn to his mouth. "Ahoy on the British frigate."

"We hear you, Captain," came the reply from the Bridge of the British ship. "Are you ready to put them over?"

"We have fourteen of your airmen to transfer. We also have one of our crewmen who was badly wounded in the rescue. We want to transfer him, also, and ask that you get medical assistance as soon as possible."

"Jolly good. We have a surgeon on board the cruiser that is standing by to take our transferees. We are in your debt, submariners."

"We are glad to be of service. We appreciate your meeting us here so we can get back onto station."

The fourteen airmen were helped into the boat. Seaman Jacobs, who had been strapped into a bunk bed, was carefully handed across from the tank tops to the boat. The British sailors pushed away from the submarine and headed back to their ship.

"We would appreciate your contacting our SubPac command at Pearl Harbor once you have cleared this area. We are returning to the duty station for another five days. Then we will be heading home."

"Jolly good, Captain. We will so inform you command." The Captain of the British frigate returned the salutes of the airmen as they came up the ladder to the deck of the frigate. Then he turned and saluted the submarine.

Captain Emerson and XO Thomas returned the salute. The two details were securing the forward deck and gun, and going below. As soon as the hatch was closed and word was received that it was secured, Emerson called for standard speed on a compass bearing of 250 degrees. He also authorized the charging of the batteries.

Skip was pleased that the British had agreed to make contact with SubPac. This would mean that he would not have to break radio silence to make his report, but would get the word back to Pearl Harbor. As radio technology advanced, there were concerns that two separate listening posts could get a bearing on a transmission and create form those two bearings a triangulation that could locate the source of the transmission.

CHAPTER TWENTY-FIVE

Joy reigned supreme at the headquarters of the Submarine Command, Pacific. They had just received the communications from the British Flotilla about the fourteen British airmen rescued by the U.S.S. Snook, and about Seaman Jacobs who was recovering well after his chest surgery aboard a British cruiser. Jacobs would be taken to the hospital at Okinawa for transfer back to Hawaii.

Admiral Pennington, Captain Brannigan, and Commander Walker were meeting in the Admiral's office. Phillip Brannigan and Jim Walker were explaining the press releases that had been sent out to date. Walker had brought the complete record of articles by the AP and UPI, as well as the local Honolulu Breeze. Adding eight more rescues would not only secure the record for the Snook but would add a broader interest of the allies since the most recent were of British airmen. The Chief Yeoman in charge of Admiral Pennington's personal staff, knocked once and entered carrying two telegraph messages which he handed to the Admiral. Pennington read them out loud.

To The President of the United States and the Secretary of War

I convey my personal thanks and the gratitude of all British subjects, for the courageous deeds of your U.S.S. SNOOK in the rescue of fourteen British Airmen. We should like to extend personal honors to the Captain and crew at an appropriate time.

With great gratitude,
Winston Churchill, Prime Minister

and
Secretary of War
Commander in Chief, Pacific Fleet
Commander, Submarine Forces, Pacific

Extraordinary efforts by extraordinary Naval personnel. Extend my gratitude and those of all United States citizens. I shall join the Congress in awarding the Congressional Medal of Honor to the Commander of U.S.S. SNOOK and such other appropriate honors to the crew.
Best,
Franklin D. Roosevelt, President

"Lets see that these messages get distributed to the press as soon as possible. This is indeed significant to all of us. The Snook will become the symbol for all the submarines in the Pacific."

"We want to interview Seaman Jacobs as soon as possible, too," inserted Brannigan. "His story will add an appropriate personal side to all this. It should not be difficult to keep the crescendo up until the return of the Snook. The Brits confirmed that Emerson told them he wanted five more days on patrol before they head back here to the barn."

"Splendid job. My thanks to both of you for the management of this media event." Admiral Pennington's attention was drawn to his intercom. Brannigan and Walker left the Admiral's office feeling very good about what they were doing for all submariners. The silent service was finally getting some attention without distracting from its tasks.

Nance took the call from Commander Walker. She was overjoyed at the news and the attention being given to Skip and his crew. Walker told her about the messages from the President of the United States and the Prime Minister of Great Britain that would be on the news soon. He offered to have copies sent to her at Tripler later that afternoon'

"You will have to work hard at keeping Skip's feet on the ground when he returns," said Jim Walker. "He and his crew are going to get more media attention that any other sub crew in history. And they deserve every bit of it.

"They are going to symbolize everything that submariners stand for.

The side benefits are that we will get more voluntary transfers into our service right at a time when more submarines are coming out of the shipyards and crews will be needed."

Nance was more interested in the personal matters. "When will they get back? Are they still on schedule?"

"Yes," responded Jim Walker. "They will get back just about as planned. Maybe even a day or so earlier. We will keep you apprised of that. All of the plans for their return are set. We are counting on you to be a big part of the return and ceremonies."

"I'm ready at any time, Commander. And thanks for this call." Nance hung up the phone and could hardly wait to share her news with her associates. By the end of the day, the entire hospital community had become aware of Lieutenant Nancy Jones 'fame by association.' Even the hospital administrator and chief of medical staff came by her ward to congratulate her, sure that Tripler's image would be enhanced by her presence.

Nance stopped on the way home and picked up a copy of the Breeze. There on the first page were copies of the letters that had been received by SubPac from President Roosevelt and Prime Minister Churchill. She decided to get extra copies to put away for a scrapbook in which she was going to compile all the articles and things that would help them remember the event. She had kept the dozen articles already published about the rescue missions from the Honolulu Breeze, the San Francisco Chronicle, and the Los Angeles Times. Friends at the hospital had brought her articles from the latter two papers they had gotten through the mail.

Back at ComSubPac headquarters, Jim Walker and his staff were working through the details for the receptions and awards ceremonies. There were military bands to be scheduled, catering of meals to be arranged, and award certificates to be completed by the base calligrapher. Award medals were picked up from the supply depot and arrangement was made for wooden bleachers to be set up at the finger pier where the Snook would be docking. Programs were published for both award ceremonies.

Press kits were assembled with copies of the programs and examples of the certificates. These Press Kits and passes were sent to offices of the AP and UPI bureau chiefs and to the Honolulu Breeze. Commander Walker was proud of his staff and their knowledge of what it took to pull all the pieces together for a smooth public image.

He joined his staff at daily meetings to discuss the status of preparations and to identify any problems. Lt. King mentioned the need for a staff photographer at one of these meetings. "The press members will not attend all the events and they are not all adept photographers. They often hire a different photographer for each article they do. And there is a need for continuity of quality pictures." It had finally been decided to hire a freelance photographer who would be on call to the SubPac staff and would cover all the events. Lt. King agreed to contact the press to make arrangements for pictures to be circulated, and to make sure they knew their photographers were welcome.

On Thursday morning, Commander Walker was summoned to Captain Brannigan's office. As he entered, he could sense the serious mood of the day. Commander Fleming, the Submarine Fleet Engineering Officer, was sitting at the conference table awaiting Phil Brannigan who was on the telephone. Fred Fleming greeted Jim Walker and motioned to the table. Jim filled his coffee cup from the service set at the sideboard.

Phil Brannigan finished his call and came to the table to join Fred and Jim. "Gentlemen, we have a problem. We have just received a communication from the British Flotilla that they cannot make contact with the Snook. After the rendezvous three days ago, they have been trying to radio Snook for the past 24 hours. They are getting no response. They contacted us to see if we had pulled Snook off patrol early."

"Do we know," said Fred Fleming, "if they have tested their equipment to make sure they are transmitting?"

"Yes. They say they have tested their transmission with another ship. Fred, if Snook realized that it had a problem with its emergency band receivers, would it make contact with the flotilla or us?"

"That is standard operating procedure, Phil. They run a test mode every couple of hours if they have not had contact otherwise. They also run a backup receiver in case one goes out. They get a visual meter indication of their transmissions. If they detect a problem with the transmission, they are to come up at their earliest opportunity and radio Pearl Harbor so we can contact the fleet."

"I know that there are a lot of reasons we may not have heard, but I am worried. The fleet command reports a lot of enemy ships in that area of operation. The Japanese are trying to alter our bombing raids by cutting off the lifeguard operations. The Carrier group is starting an effort to clear out the enemy ships, but that is just getting started."

"Captain, there are a lot of things that could have happened," Fleming said. "We need to trust in Skip Emerson and his crew. They have come through a lot, just as we did when we were out there. They may have had a major communications break down. It is even possible, though not probable, that they do not know they have a problem. I say, let's wait and see. When are they due to send us a message?"

"Our log indicates they should start their return transit in two more days." Said Walker. "They are supposed to send us a message as they start that transit, after they have cleared the operations area. We should be concerned, but I agree that we have to let time play out on this."

"I know you two are right, but I don't feel good about this. We have so much riding on the safe return of Snook. Paramount, of course, is my concern for the personnel that are on board. Jim, ask our communications officer to keep close tabs on anything relating to the operational area. Also ask her to monitor the British Flotilla that we are working with. Perhaps they will hear something they may not otherwise report. I need for you to prepare a draft response to the British admiralty. I'd like to be brief and simple."

"Do I say anything to Lt. Jones about this?" asked Walker.

"No, it is too early," responded Brannigan. "But keep that thought for us. If we have not heard anything in two days, I want you to revisit that question. I want for us to be straight with Nurse Jones, just as she has been with us. In the meantime, push ahead with our plans for their return.

"And Fred, I want your engineering team to simulate this situation to see if you can come up with anything we have not discussed. That is all, gentlemen. Let's plan to meet at 0900 tomorrow to see where we are."

Phil Brannigan went upstairs to brief the Admiral on the situation.

They agreed to wait and see, and to hope for the best for Emerson and his crew.

Later that morning, Captain Brannigan sent a coded message to the admiralty of the British Flotilla 17 stating that the U.S.S. Snook had not been recalled and was presumed to be operating in accordance with its instructions. It reminded the Brits that the emergency communications system was new and not fully tested, and suggested that the submarine might not be able to contact the flotilla, or even use its antenna system, because of enemy action in the area.

At 0800 on Friday morning, Commander Walker was sitting in the office of Lieutenant Sue James, the SubPac Communications Officer. "What have we heard?" he inquired.

"We dispatched the command's response to the British Flotilla at noon yesterday. There has been no further communications from them. We are monitoring their frequencies but the traffic has been normal. Likewise, there has been no unusual traffic from the operating area, other than fleet reports that the allied aircraft are beating back the enemy warships that had invaded the area. Those ships now seem to have retreated and the bombing runs have resumed."

"We will appreciate your continued monitoring, Sue. We are a little concerned about the Snook, which should be sending a message as they start their return transit in the next twenty-four hours."

"Will do, Jim. That's our job. We are always glad to be of service. I'll leave messages for you and Captain Brannigan should we hear anything related to Snook."

The meeting with Brannigan was a short one. Fleming reported that no problems had been experienced with the emergency frequency receivers that were maintained in the Radio Shop on the Sub Base. They had been purchased at the same time as those aboard the Snook. His engineers agreed that if there was a problem, it was most likely with the antenna system.

"Sue James, our Communications Officer, tells me the enemy warships have been chased out of the operating area," reported Jim Walker. "If Snook was being held down by those warships, they should now be able to come up to communications depth. The next 24 hours will, indeed, tell us if we have a real problem."

"O.K., gentlemen. I hope that neither of you had plans for the weekend. I think we had better plan to meet tomorrow at around noon. I'll have some lunch catered in. We should have a better feel for the situation by then."

Fleming had one last comment. "You both know that we may not know anything tomorrow. If Snook has a major electronics problem, they may not be able to get word to us until they can signal someone on the surface. Or, I suppose, until they return to Pearl Harbor."

Later that Friday afternoon, a communications was received from Flotilla 17 indicating they were ending their action in the assigned area. It thanked the Submarine Forces, Pacific, for the support and valiant efforts of the Snook in the rescue of its airmen. It ended with a thought for the Snook, hoping that the lifeguard would swim back safely to its base.

Captain Brannigan had hoped that the meeting of the three officers at SubPac Saturday morning would be preceded by a telephone call telling him that Snook had made contact. Then their meeting could be focused on the plans for the receptions and ceremonies. But such was not the case.

"I stopped by the Communications Center on the way up," stated Walker. "I just had to be sure that any last minute messages would be in our hands. Nothing has changed."

"Well, we will just proceed with our plans." Phil Brannigan was visibly concerned and seemed to be detached from the conversation. His thoughts were elsewhere for that moment. "I think I had better contact Lt. Jones to let her know there is a communications problem. I don't want to upset her, but I think we owe her the same respect she has shown us."

"Please remind her of other subs that have limped back to port late," inserted Fleming. "We must keep the faith."

"Of course," agreed Walker. "We must remain confident that Snook will return. But I agree, Phil. There should be contact with Nance Jones. Would you like for me to make that contact?"

"Thanks, Jim, but I think it should be me," responded Brannigan. "I will keep everything as casual as possible. You both know that. But we had better start thinking about how to manage the news if it is not good. We have a lot of national attention building toward the return of this submarine. And thanks to both of you for breaking in to your weekend plans for this meeting. I hope you can enjoy your families for the rest of it. If I hear anything, I will give you a call. You will be able to reach me at home, or by leaving a message at the Comm Center."

After Jim Walker and Fred Fleming left, Phil Brannigan sat quietly in his chair. He stared out the window toward the Submarines Base below, and the azure Pacific Ocean beyond. But he saw nothing of the beauty. His mind recalled other times when submarines were overdue. Each was an agony for him until the fate was decided. Some returned to Pearl Harbor days after they were due to arrive. Some showed up at Guam or Midway where temporary repairs could be made. Some were never heard from again.

He picked up his telephone and dialed Nance's apartment.

EPILOGUE

The U.S.S. Snook was never heard from again. Research by Clay Blair, Jr. indicates that the U.S.S. Snook was ordered on April 12, 1945, to lifeguard for a British carrier strike. On April 20, the British officer commanding the force called upon the Snook to rescue an aviator when his plane went down in Snook's vicinity. The British officer was unable to make contact. Nothing more was ever heard from the U.S.S. Snook. A search of Japanese records after the war revealed no clue as to her loss.

The United States Navy submarines contributed greatly to the success in the Pacific, but they paid heavily for that success. Fifty-two submarines were lost, carrying a total of 374 officers and 3131 enlisted men, and were proclaimed as "still on patrol" by Vice Admiral C. A. Lockwood, Jr. the Commander of Submarine Forces, 1943-1946.

It is to these brave men that we dedicate this book.

ABOUT THE AUTHOR

So why am I writing a historic novel about U.S. submarines in the WWII Pacific Theatre? Though I served my country a decade after WWII, I was stationed on a submarine that was built before that war ended and was the same class of submarine as the U.S.S. Snook.

I am a member of several submarine veteran organizations: United States Submarine Veterans, Inc. is open to current submariners as well as veterans of any era; World War II Submarine Veterans: and the Naval Submarine League—members of which have encouraged me. John Andersen, past national treasurer of USSVI, has shown keen interest. CAPT. John Peters, past president of USSVI was a skipper on a WWII submarine out of Pearl Harbor. CAPT. Peters met with me in Hawaii last summer and encouraged my efforts.

In the past several years, I have volunteered as an advisor to the United States Navy Recruiting Station in Los Angeles, California and have met many of the young men who are serving on newer classes of nuclear submarines. These men have given great encouragement in expressing their interest in what submariners really accomplished during WWII.

As a youngster who could not afford college in Iowa, I joined the U.S. Navy in California to establish my residency so that I could attend college after serving my enlistment. Some National Guard experience while I was in high school gave me a kick-start in advancing my Naval career and I became Interior Communications Petty Officer First Class, IC1 (SS) in three years, something the current enlistees can no longer attain in their first enlistment. Though I now have four university degrees, I still treasure my experiences as a United States Navy submariner.

I take full responsibility for writing this historic novel. I have researched it through primary and secondary sources; the Naval Archives provided copies of Patrol Reports and Log Books that served, along with interviews, as a primary source; non-fiction authors such as Clay Blair, Jr. have provided great sets of information about the efforts of our valiant warriors under the sea. I purposely have used fictional characters to protect the private lives of those men who served on the U.S.S. Snook. Any similarities to persons, living or dead, are purely coincidental and are the creation of my mind.

I want to thank my wife, Jilonne Menefee, for reading and critiquing my work. I want to thank Janet Kuramata who did an amazing job of editing my work and making suggestions for a "better read."

Lifeguard on Duty
Gerald R. Menefee

Breinigsville, PA USA
30 March 2011
258758BV00001B/104/P